*The Broughty Souls*..................  .2

Chapter one ........................... ................................4

Chapter two.................................................................13

Chapter three .............................................................27

Chapter four................................................................53

Chapter five.................................................................67

Chapter six..................................................................78

Chapter seven..........................................................116

Chapter eight............................................................141

Chapter nine.............................................................162

Chapter ten ..............................................................181

# The Broughty Souls

Broughty Ferry is a small Scottish town nestled between Monifieth and her larger neighbour Dundee. The town is situated on the banks of the River Tay. As an important coastal town, Broughty has always been involved with the fishing industry and more recently has acted as a harbour for oil rigs brought in for maintenance from the North Sea. These are an interesting sight just a short way offshore. Both industries have provided many jobs and have played a huge part in boosting the local economy. There is a 'RNLI' lifeboat station strategically situated on the Broughty beach. For decades brave crews have been involved in many rescues. Sadly, there have been numerous failed attempts due to the unforgiving nature of both the North Sea and the treacherous currents out in the Tay. Many local men and women have lost their lives attempting to rescue stricken vessels of all types.
The lifeboat house is positioned so that it can head off out to sea, or in the opposite direction to the River Tay, winding inland past the City of Dundee. In recent years, archaeologists have made discoveries that suggest there was a settlement on this land in the prehistoric period. The small hamlet as it originally was, grew in size to a large town due to a growing success in fishing and whaling. Broughty was involved in all the Anglo-Scottish wars due to the strategic location of the town on the banks of the river, with Broughty Castle being founded in 1490 by King James IV. This was an attempt by the Scots to fend off an ever-increasing threat from the English Navy.

During the 19th century, a great deal of money and wealth was made by Jute Barons who traded with the cloth. These entrepreneurs of the time built wonderful mansions in the traditional Scottish Baroque style. Today, many of these impressive buildings still exist and have been converted into plush apartments and posh hotels. Broughty is very popular with holiday makers and people in search of adventure, with many venturing out to the surrounding hills and mountains. These can be especially unpredictable in the winter and sadly to this day, the unpredictable nature of the weather claims many lives.

For all the reasons mentioned, Broughty is not without its tragedy. Due to the towns involvement in war and the constant need for fishing out at sea, many lives have been lost. One such local tragedy was when the Tay Rail Bridge collapsed. This infamous disaster took the lives of some 79 souls. On that fateful December night back in 1879, the region had suffered the worst weather for years. A fierce storm caused part of the bridge to collapse, causing a crossing train to plunge into the murky depths below.

There are many local tales about hauntings. These range from spectres seen in ruins, to Roman soldiers who disappear through walls. There are tales of 'The Green Lady' who walks the battlements at Claypotts Castle. Others involve sightings of ghostly boats seen lit up in the river that suddenly vanish without a trace. Others say that on the anniversary of the rail disaster screams can be heard amongst the howling winds out in the Tay, often accompanied by strange lights.

# Chapter one

It was spring of 2008. Bruce, a middle-aged man just a few weeks away from 48, had recently taken on an office-based role as a Staff Sergeant in the army. After joining from school at 16, he had served 28 years; a long career. He never married or had children, concentrating on his military career. He chose The Royal Dragoon Guard's, or RDG's as they are more commonly known. His father Alec was in the same regiment during the late 1960s but sadly got injured by a roadside bomb in 76, whilst on patrol in Northern Ireland. He survived but lost his right hand and lower left leg, just below the knee.

Things at home in Cove Bay Aberdeen were tough enough at this time, but after his father was medically discharged life got very difficult. Wounded soldiers were lucky to receive a couple of thousand pounds compensation back then, and for a man in his 20's unemployable due to the severity of his injuries, the money lasted a matter of months. Alec drank a great deal in a bid to drown out his past misfortune. This led to arguments with Sheila his wife and on many occasions the police were called due to the noise from arguing and the crashing of objects being thrown. In Autumn of 81, just five years after Alec was so brutally wounded, he took his own life. His body was discovered hanging in the garden shed by a neighbour's gardener, who saw and heard suspicious movements. Alec was just 33 years old.

Bruce himself was a carbon copy of his father, six feet tall athletic with dark blonde hair. He was good looking for 48, apart from a burn scar on his right cheek- a few inches long. This was caused by a ricochet when a sniper fired at him fortunately missing. The bullet clipped the corner of a wall during a patrol in Bosnia in the mid 90's.

In 2006 he was deployed to Helmand Province in Afghanistan. Shortly after he was promoted to the rank of Staff Sergeant. His unit was armoured and took delivery of modified vehicles. These were upgraded with the latest 'anti RPG' (Rocket Propelled Grenade) bars, that greatly reduced the number of ever-increasing casualties. However, the underbelly of such vehicles were still vulnerable.

The troops were better protected from their recent exchanges with the Taliban. Bruce had been involved in some of the heaviest fighting. After many enemy 'contacts' he came close to following in his father's footsteps whilst out on patrol one chilly winters morning. The route they were on a few miles out of a forward operating base in Helmand had seen numerous ambushes and IED attacks; (Improvised Explosive Devises).

On that fateful morning, his vehicle triggered an IED causing their newly delivered Mastiff vehicle to lift into the air a few feet almost breaking in half. His driver Corporal Nathan Hill died instantly. Bruce and three others were miraculously thrown clear suffering minor injuries.

The death of his good friend Nathan, 'Nuts' as he was known had a profound impact on Bruce. They had joined the army at the same time and went through basic training together. He would find himself waking up in the night with the sweats, as his dead pal would be stood a few feet away from him. Moments later he would disappear. This happened on tour and at home, but each time it never failed to frighten him. This wasn't his first paranormal encounter and certainly wouldn't be his last.

Eventually, after his last tour of Afghanistan in late 2007 as rank of Staff Sergeant, he undertook office-based duties at the age of 47. After numerous deployments, he found the change boring but all the same pleasant. He was based at Leuchars Station near Fife Scotland, where he had bought a small apartment that required significant updating with some of his deployment bonuses. The small two-bed property was on the west end of town, not far from Claypotts Castle.

He purchased the apartment intending on living there after the work was done. However, he decided to let it out to bring in enough money to pay the mortgage. It had been converted from a handsome four-bedroom 1920s era house. He also had a small two bed house just outside of camp. This was a military home that he rented through his salary. This was his main home conveniently situated just a five-minute cycle to his office on a good day.

A few months after his father's untimely death, his mother hit the bottle hard. She struggled with new relationships, never able to move on from her loss of Alec. Bruce would often lay awake at night listening to his mother's sobs, as she reminisced about good times with him. She bumped along in and out of part-time jobs trying to make ends meet.

Sheila always had a brave face and was known for her beaming smile, but inside she never recovered from the loss of Alec. Sadly, in December of 97 while Bruce was deployed in Sarajevo Bosnia, he received the grim news that his mother had been killed in a car crash. The post-mortem revealed she had been four times over the legal limit. She had taken the car out after an evening of drinking. She spun the car off the road, down a ravine and into a freezing river; Brig O' Dee. The official reason for death: 'by drowning.'

Bruce was granted compassionate leave that December. He flew home to her funeral and stayed at the family home for a few weeks. There was no inheritance at all. Most people at that time rented from the council as did his parents and their parents before them. He had a decent living quarter on camp at Leuchars base, so usually he would only visit his mother briefly while on leave. Once the funeral was over and friends and family had gone, he was left alone. After a couple of weeks sifting through her possessions and sorting out the usual household items, it was time to leave the property. The council were booked in to do a deep clean. Then he would leave his family home behind for good.

On the penultimate night in the house, he was exhausted. He had hired a van to take all manner of things to the local tip. Back then the tip was a quick affair. The older people amongst us will remember backing up to a waste height concrete wall, before chucking over everything from garden, household, food, pet waste, sofas, drawer units the lot. This melee of unwanted waste would crash down to an enormous stinking heap below, exploding and scattering around three or four poor sods as they attempted to sift through the detritus.

There was a certain 'final' feeling attached to throwing recognisable items over that wall. He had filled black bags full of his late mother's clothes. Back in the day as they say, the advent of charity donations at such shops wasn't a thing. People would quite frankly not care one bit. The common consensus wasn't to worry about saving the world. Recycling was for the rag-n-bone man who turned up with a megaphone twice yearly.

Bruce got to finally rest on the one item he had left to get rid of; a three-seater cream leather settee. He had thought about trying to stuff it into his roomy Peugeot 406 estate but decided it was too good to dump. His mother had paid a small fortune for it. She took out one of many high interest loans paying it off weekly at the front door. At that time, 'gone-legit' loan- shark companies certainly were a God send for her.

The following morning, an old family friend was due to pick it up for £60; not great but a decent amount for a well-worn- in settee. The magnolia paint on the walls in the lounge were covered in stained square shapes. These were the shadows caused by years of smoking where pictures were once mounted. The room seemed to echoe once emptied despite having a decent light blue carpet with underlay.

He seemed to slide about on the huge settee, recalling how his mother used to polish it with pledge. There was an old military sleeping bag stuffed in his car boot, used mainly for fishing trips. Sprawled out on the settee in his toasty bag, he had a 'What Car' magazine for his entertainment. He did have a mobile back then, but they didn't offer all the features you can readily access today. Back then reading was very much the entertainment of an evening. Lying in bed swiping through endless amounts of pointless but entertaining reels hadn't yet become a way of life. There was a small table lamp plugged in at a corner of the room. This offered enough light for him to read. The TV had gone in for repair just a week or so before his mother passed away, and knowing there was going to be a bill to pay, he didn't bother contacting the repair company.

It was that evening that things took a creepy turn. He was nodding off in and out of sleep, occasionally waking to wipe off another stream of dribble from his chin. He could hear a movement upstairs. The sound seemed like a cat jumping off a bed. They had kept a cat ten years earlier but Fluffy came to an awful end, after falling asleep in an engine compartment. She lost her tail when it got caught up in the fan belt. That morning when the unsuspecting neighbour started the engine, Fluffy was drawn into the fan belt leading to her gruesome end.

The noise happened again, the exact same. Startled this time he sat up staring at the ceiling. At first, he wasn't bothered until the sound repeated itself. This time he heard a startling clunk from a door latch closing upstairs.

He slipped his legs out of his toasty bag and sat up on the edge of the settee. He looked up daring not to breathe and then 'THUMP! THUMP!' This time he stood up and froze to the spot. "HELLO!" he shouted out, staring at the gloomy hallway door. The sudden realisation that he was calling out to a sound in an empty house at silly o-clock at night, caused his heart to race. However, he was no stranger to terrifying situations in the army and was an expert at keeping his cool.

This was different. The sounds stopped. Nothing but deathly quiet.

'What shall I do now?' he thought. He decided to investigate upstairs. Sliding his old tatty part-fluffy slippers on, he pushed the hallway door open and headed to the bottom of the stairs. He reached in for a switch in the hall and flicked the upstairs landing light on.

Once again: "HELLO! IS SOMEONE THERE?" he called out.... nothing.

He grabbed a handrail and slowly climbed the stairs. As he got to the middle, he peered around through a couple of spindles. He focused on the main front bedroom door. He could see that it was slightly ajar. The other three, a bathroom and two other bedroom doors were closed. 'Did I close them all?' he thought. Pretty certain he had done so; it worried him further that the door was open. He reached the top of the stairs and stood at the door. Gripping the cool brass knob, he pushed it open. It swung right around thudding the inner wall.

He flicked the light switch and looked around. The room was decorated in a garish pink and blue Roses. To match his late mother's awful taste was a threadbare jade green carpet. He stepped inside. Over in the far-right hand corner, at the bottom of a wide front window was an object. It was a broken picture frame. He turned it over making sure he didn't cut himself on the cracked glass. He was immediately greeted by two happy smiles. They were both holding a cigarette. He mused at the picture that reminded him of his childhood. It was his mother and her sister Aunty Alice.

They were in the bar at the hotel Alice had bought back in the late 80s, The Dunella Hotel in Broughty Ferry. Bruce had not seen his aunty for a few years. Sheila and Alice did keep in touch, but his mother was far too keen on the booze and Alice was very busy running the hotel. Alice and Uncle Stanley had bought the hotel cheaply in the late 80's. They had poured their life savings into Dunella, as the dilapidated building required a refurbishment. The project went very well, and they re-opened to the public in 91. Just seven years later Uncle Stanley died suddenly, succumbing to a massive heart attack. He had been a relatively fit man in his seventies. Stanley had never smoked and only tended to drink on special occasions.

Alice fought on at the hotel. To help her along she hired a great General Manager. As far as Bruce knew at this point, her business was still doing well.

He left the room taking another final look around. Clutching the picture, he carefully went back downstairs and settled in his sleeping bag. The noises he had heard were unusual, but he assumed they were made by the picture frame falling off the windowsill. He was exhausted from sorting out the house and doing the trips to the dump. As he dosed in and out of sleep, he wondered about the noises. There wasn't a window open to cause any draft. And the cat jumping sound causing a definite thud? He thought about that too but eventually succumbed to tiredness and fell asleep.

It came as a bit of a relief when morning came. He was lying in his toasty sleeping bag watching the early morning light fill the room.

Suddenly there was a loud knock at the front door.

He jumped, startled and rubbed his weary eyes. The knocking repeated as he quickly pulled up his jeans.

"BE THERE IN A SEC!" he called out.

He went to the front door and opened it up. There stood a tall man, wearing a black woolly beanie, a dark bomber jacket and jeans covered in holes and splodges of paint. His beard was a wiry mix of black and grey. The pointed nature of the beard reminded him of a wizard from a fantasy novel. The man replied in a deep voice which was a very broad Aberdonian accent. "Morning Bruce, I'm a little earlier than planned, is now a good time for collection?" he asked.

"Yes, of course Jack, good... I mean come in. I just woke up sorry I'm half asleep come in," he said. He turned and waved his hand at someone by the gate. He was a friend who came along to help load up the settee.

"I appreciate this I really do. Your mother used to love this settee, the colour especially," said Jack.

"Oh, um yes, she did. You knew her well?"

Jack moved to one end of the settee and was about to lift it up, his buddy already had his end off the floor. He hesitated and stopped for a moment. "I was acquainted with your mother; we met at the spiritualist church doon the road."

"Spiritualist church?" asked Bruce.

"Aye, The Bon-Accord spiritualist and healing centre; you didna ken your mother was a member?"

Bruce stroked his stubble, nodding slightly. He had no idea that his mother was into that sort of thing.

Jack and his buddy lifted the settee up and took it out, loading it onto a small van. He returned to the house and stood at the door. "Great all done. HELLO BRUCE?" he called out.

Bruce appeared, still thinking about his mother's secret association with the Bon-Accord.

"Come in a moment. How long was she attending your Church?"

"Well now, let me think a minute. She had drink issues I ken that much. I'd say aboot end of 92, yes that's right. I'd say a good few years."

"Oh, ok that's news to me. I was away a lot. I knew mum was a bit lonely and I didn't make the effort to see her nearly enough."

"If it's any comfort Bruce your mother used to come in twice weekly with her sister," he said.

"Ah sister, that would be my Aunty Alice. I thought they were too busy for each other."

"On the contrary Bruce, your aunty was a big believer, and your mother started to get into it big time." A loud double honk from the vans horn blared from outside; his buddy was getting impatient.

"BE THERE IN A MIN," called Jack. He took out a small wad of fivers and placed them into Bruce's hand. He closed his hand up tightly and locked eyes with Bruce.

"Your aunty used to do séances up at Dunella. Your mother, she wanted to speak one more time with your father." Bruce let go of his hand, startled at that news. His heart starting to race thanks to that revelation. Jack headed off up the path. At the garden gate he turned to face him and said: "Your aunty she had a gift, as did your mother, you might too it's usually in the blood," he said.

Alone again, he carried on securing the house, locking windows and turned off the electric. He couldn't shake off what Jack had told him. His mother and aunty had dabbled in contacting the dead at Dunella. Did they contact Alec his dad or not? Only Alice would have that answer, and he didn't want anything to do with it.

He eventually returned to Barracks carrying out his now office based soldiering duties. He had no reason to contact his aunty and wanted nothing to do with the secret he learned from Jack. That revelation had had spooked him.

# Chapter two

It was 2008. Bruce was back in camp at Leuchars. He was settling down into his daily routine as a 'staffy,' (army slang for Staff Sergeant). The pay was good and having no dependents as such had enabled him to shove a few quid in the bank. This money and the extra earned from deployment bonuses are what he used to buy his Broughty apartment.

The humdrum of the office didn't always bode well with him. Most of his day was taken up triaging admin duties and sorting out warrants for arrest, usually due to soldiers going AWOL, (absent without leave). The war in Afghanistan had demanded a great deal from young soldiers. They were witnessing horrendous situations almost daily and by the latter end of 2008 the war had escalated. By that point in the conflict 51 British soldiers had been killed in 2008 alone. Many were returning home on leave and not reporting back to unit.

One Friday afternoon, with his paperwork squared away, there was a knock on the office door.

"HELLO, COME IN!" he called.

The door swung open, and a very smartly dressed officer walked in, sporting number two dress with peaked cap in one hand, clutching a brown envelope in the other.

"Staff Sergeant Gordon?" he asked.

"Yes erm... sir that's me. How may I help?"

He entered the office, heading for the seat opposite Bruce. He was a tall man, fairly portly about six feet tall, and looked about 40 years old. He had dark hair slightly balding on top. He also bore a scar under his left eye, another common indication of an experienced soldier. This one though was an officer wearing four medals on his top left pocket.

He took out a cigarette and without asking lit it up, taking a long drag on it.

Bruce took out a glass ashtray from his top drawer and placed it on the desktop. He had given up smoking a year earlier but kept his ashtray as a memento of his achievement. He sat back in his chair intrigued, not quite knowing what to say.

"How can I be of service? Captain...Major?"

"I'm Major Philby, I work for the Adjutants General Corps. I'm here on business for the Padre Office."

"Padre, are you a Vicar?"

"Not quite, I deliver all sorts of news for the army, usually the bad kind these days. I spend a lot of time delivering news of a death to a family typically."

"So why are you here? I don't know of any one close serving, and I don't have a wife or kids either," he asked. Major Philby placed the envelope on the desk. It had a large white sticker on it. Stamped with:

**DELIVER BY HAND.**

Bruce took hold of it and hesitated.

"I am sorry to announce this, but your Aunt Alice has passed," he said, as calm as a daisy.

The major stood up and placed his hat on, stepping back one pace and saluted. He turned to the door and stopped for a moment.

"Sorry about the news old boy. I know that she had no other immediate family. Everything you need to know and do, it's in the letter. Good day Staff Sergeant."

Alone again, Bruce felt a little numb. He wanted to open it and find out everything. At the same time, he knew that if he was the only immediate close family member, then what he was about to find out could have significant life-changing consequences.

He reached into the drawer once again, pulling out a long silver envelope opener. He slotted it in the end and tore it across. Taking out the letter, he opened it slowly and respectfully.

*Spire Solicitors Dundee*
*Probate Specialists*
*26/04/2008*

*Dear Mr Bruce Gordon,*

*With the utmost condolence for your loss and respect at this very sensitive time, I have been appointed to deal with and complete the delivery of the estate, concerning the late:*
*Mrs Alice Dogherty. We understand that this time is very sensitive. Please do contact me when the time is right for you,*

*Yours sincerely,*

### Kenneth Campbell

"Am I taking on a hotel?" he said to himself. He put the letter away and considered what had just happened. He knew he only had a couple of years left to work in the army, with most long serving soldiers retiring aged 50. This would be a great opportunity.

The Dunella Hotel, established in 1828, was originally a grand Georgian building. It was originally built as many were, with the wealth amassed from the Jute trade, (a kind of hessian) fisheries and textiles. These were all huge industries at the time. Dundee prospered in the early 19th century and Broughty Ferry was chosen as a haven for the wealthy. Many thousands would flock to the town and stay for a vacation and business trips. Consequently, many of the larger private dwellings became guest rooms offering an overnight stay with breakfast, the forerunners for BnB's.

Dunella spent her early years in and out of fortune. If the local economy was struggling, the guest rooms were empty, making little to no money. In prosperous times, the rooms were packed and Dunella always made her owners wealthy.

By the late 1970s the hotel had fallen into disrepair. Owners came, invested little and consequently the business would fail. That was until 1987. Alice and Stanley had been looking to invest. They had prospered from running a medium sized building company. Parts of Dundee had been run down for decades and Stanley's maintenance firm expanded into the building industry.

Many pre-war tenements were demolished, leaving in their wake a great opportunity for companies engaged in the building boom of the eighties. Small companies expanded and grew into successful businesses. It was summer of 87. Stanley had been winding down his company, selling off assets and several successful contracts. One of them was a maintenance contract that covered hotels. Dunella had often been visited by Stanley, under the name: D.M.S. (Dundee Maintenance Services).

He had always admired the old building with its grand entrance, leading to several fine rooms that had been converted and improved over the years. In the early eighties, investment companies came and went. DMS would carry out basic maintenance at Dunella. That typically involved repairs to leaking pipes, particularly numerous, nipping up gas pipe leaks in the out-dated kitchen, and re-wiring most of the bed. This was designed to improve the advance in technology, such as early cable TV.

Stanley was now in his early 60s. He had wanted to retire for a while, but the opportunity became serious when one sunny day in August 87, a letter arrived at the office. It turned out that the accountancy firm they hired to do the books, were under investigation for fraud. D.M.S. were facing an unpaid debt to The Inland Revenue amounting to £32,000. This was a shock and the company although cash rich, could not meet the demand. Stanley had one concrete option. He had to sell up. The company was one of three that monopolised the sector.

It turned out that a local entrepreneur from Dusseldorf in Germany had shown an interest in such firms. In the early eighties, Germany had undergone a huge rebuilding and modernisation programme. Much of the destruction caused from World War Two, had created a tsunami of investment. In fact, the popular TV show 'Alf Wiedersehen Pet' was based on that period. Tens of thousands from the U.K with skills such as carpentry, plumbing and electrical flocked to Germany. The benefit of such a huge economic migration meant that firms operating at home had huge opportunity due to the lack of skilled manpower left behind.

It was a miracle in waiting. The offer from the German company, a generous £95,000 was enough to sell, pay off debts and have a good amount left over to either run off into the sunset, or invest in a new venture. Just a few months after they had first been contacted by the German, the deal was sealed. The company was sold, and the debts were paid off in full.

It was now a cold January in 88, when Dunella was up for sale, once again. The local paper 'The Evening Telegraph' had a decent four-page property spread at the back.

Stanley and Alice had been enjoying a trip to a little cabin he had built out at Blair Gowrey, when one morning whilst sat eating breakfast he noticed the hotel for sale. They decided to put an offer in to purchase it. With a little luck and plenty of negotiating on the price, due to the poor state of the building, the offer was accepted. Four months later the deal was completed. Dunella was purchased for an under-market value of £42,950, around £350,000 in today's money. This left plenty in the kitty for a refurbishment.

They were now the proud new owners of The Dunella Hotel. Bruce tucked the letter into a top pocket and sat back. He looked around the office, momentarily staring out across an empty parade square. On every wall hung a picture of his stages during his career. Mostly the typical type, with up to 50 soldiers stood on benches, the front rank reserved for command ranks with hands outstretched onto their knees. He glanced across his desk at a couple of picture frames. One had a picture of him with his best pal that was killed in Afghanistan. They were stood in front of a desert cam coloured Mastif. Just three weeks after the picture was taken, his best mate in that picture was killed. killed.

Bruce carried a great deal of guilt with him, due to him surviving the same explosion. The other picture was just one of his mum and dad, taken back in the late 70's at a bar in the Wirral near Liverpool. They used to go camping that way, with dad visiting old army friends usually. Not satisfied with his desk job, he pondered the thought of running Dunella. Was it time to go? Was it finally time to say a goodbye to all he'd known in his adult life. The career that he carved out over almost 30 years. He thought about it, a great deal, knowing that ideally, he should serve another two years to max out his pension entitlement. He would see what comes of the telephone call with Kenneth Campbell.

The next morning was a typical rainy Friday. He woke a little later than usual. He was always a punctual man with work a priority. This time, it was different. He felt a strong urge to pull a sick day. He sat at his kitchen table staring out at the rain. He scraped the last spoon or two out of his bowl of porridge, reading mail as he licked the spoon.

'That's it, I'll go in a bit late. 'Bugger it,' he thought. Glancing up at his wall clock, he realised he was going to be late as it was. The office on base was just a five-minute cycle away from his army home. He would normally leave at 8.30am, rolling in at about 8.20am...it was now 8.20am. He texted the secretary at the office reception.:

**'MORNING CHLOE, NOT LIKE ME, ALARM WASN'T SET,   BE IN ASAP, BRUCE.'**

He knew he would call the solicitor at 9am. He sat watching the clock tick by.
Swigging the last of his coffee, eventually the clock turned nine.

"Good morning, Spire, how may I help you?" a female voice answered.

"Um, hi, yes...morning, my name is Bruce...err, Bruce Gordon, can I speak to Kenneth Campbell please?"

"Yes of course, hold one moment please."

The music was awful, he had heard some 'hold' jingles that were soul destroying, but this one, a crackly version of 'Eye of the tiger,' by Survivor really didn't seem right for a solicitor's company. It seemed to take forever......finally:

"Putting you through now Mr Gordon."

He hesitated for a few moments as he was not sure what to say. The annoying jingle music stopped, followed by a brief silence.

"Mr Gordon, thank you very much for getting in touch so soon," said the voice, in a perfectly spoken broad Scottish accent.

"Yes, I thought I would see what the letter is all about you sent me?" replied Bruce.

"Ahh, yes, intriguing I assume, and out of the blue?"

"Yes, it was indeed Mr Campbell, the content suggested my late aunt may have put me in her will?"

"Yes, you are bang on Mr Gordon, there is a matter we need to discuss. Are you able to pop into the office at some point?"

He looked at the clock, it was now just after nine, he wanted to say any day is good, but he had a strong urge to find out about the will sooner.

"Actually, I have a slot today if you are able to fit me in, I know it's a little short notice."

The line fell silent, a few moments passed and then: "Great, the sooner the better, I have a cancellation for 2.30pm this afternoon if that suits you, Mr Gordon?"

"Super, I'll be there. Do I need to bring anything in particular?"

"Yes, just yourself and some I.d such as passport or driving licence will do, and a recent bill."

Bruce hung up and let out a long sigh of relief. He glanced at the clock and realised he had to contact work a second time:

'**HEY CHLOE, ME AGAIN, UNBELIEVABLE LUCK THIS MORNING, GOT AN UPSET STOMACH, PROBS BEST BE OFF TODAY.**'

He felt so awkward, especially telling a work colleague a blatant lie, a feeble one at that.

However, there was something far more pressing on the horizon, so it had to be done.

This was the first time in years that he had put something else before the army. The only time he had come away on leave was 'compassionate' for a wedding or a funeral. This time, it was very different. The way the morning had gone, it almost felt like fate was in control.

He decided to get on with a few chores around the house. There were a good few hours to burn before he set off to the solicitor's office. He wondered what to wear. For so long, weekdays meant perfectly pressed military combat trousers and top, today it would be something less obvious, perhaps a pair of black jeans and a pale blue shirt would do. One thing was for sure; he had taken a day off sick with stomach-ache, a lie that bothered him. That meant that he had to try his best not to be seen by certain people.

The accommodation on camp wasn't actually within the wire. (army slang for on base). Most of the housing was made up of flats and housing, nestling on the outskirts. However, his house was on the main rat run to the main camp gates. As the hours passed by, he found himself doing a few menial tasks. For a man that was usually based in an office all day, it seemed a nice change to be pushing a vacuum around and giving the kitchen and bathroom a once over. It was now after 12pm and he decided to make a small lunch. Nothing special, just a cheese and pickle sandwich, and a KitKat from the cupboard. He boiled the kettle and noted that he had at least a couple extra cups of coffee that morning. His nerves about the meeting starting to manifest.

Soon it was time to get ready. He did in fact choose a formal pair of trousers, dark blue but smart. He favoured a white shirt, open necked and his favourite dark brown leather shoes that you could see your face in the polished reflection. The office for Spire was about a 20-minute drive, so he had to head off shortly. The time had come; he left the front door and closed it gently, trying not to make a sound. He double checked the path at the end of his drive was clear and made a dash for his car. "So far so good," he said out loud.

He hastily entered the post code for Spire in his Tom-Tom. This was an early form of sat-nav in vehicles that were dedicated to just navigating, unlike the apps of today installed on mobile devices. Arguably the earlier sat-nav tech was better, however they did have issues updating the software and sometimes you would find yourself driving through a field that had recently become a dual carriageway.

He set off, checking carefully before he pulled out. Nobody of any significance was nearby. Bruce started to feel excited, the anticipation of receiving great news, hopefully about an inheritance. He had planned to work a further two years, but this would certainly make him reconsider. As he drove, he was already planning what he would say in his resignation letter. After almost thirty years of service, where would you start? Many veterans have come and gone, and most struggle finding a new path in 'civvy' street. He knew quite a few mates that had long since left the army, many turning to drink, suffering failed marriages due to undiagnosed PTSD. (Post traumatic stress disorder). This is a huge killer of veterans, not limited to the British armed

forces, it's a worldwide problem. For decades, soldiers would return from active duty and wonder why an exhaust back-firing in the street would cause a victim of PTSD to dive over a hedge or cower down in a foetal position. Some would only realise they had a problem when the mental images of a tour entered their minds, causing them to wake, with their hands grabbing a partner's throat. In 2008 alone there were as many as 4000 reported cases.

Some ex-military were stronger than others. Bruce was one, he never really thought about the carnage he had witnessed. In his time, he had witnessed close friends being shot, wounded or killed. He had seen the result of explosion's and sadly he'd been involved in the repatriation of the dead, retrieved from mass graves. All of which can have a profound effect on the mental well-being of military personnel, both in service and long after discharge. It is obviously an indication of strength of mind if someone is still serving after almost 30 years.

He checked the Tom-Tom; he was only two miles from his destination. He had been in some truly challenging situations before, but this time, this particular day, he felt his arm pits dampening as his anxiety level increased. Finally, he had arrived. He had five minutes to spare, seeming like eternity. Eventually, he was sitting in a pleasant reception area, picking a magazine from a pile on a side table. He browsed through them. The last time he had seen such a pile of dog-eared magazines, he was at his doctor's surgery, having an in-grown toenail looked at. He noted the headings, 'Gardeners World,' 'Vogue,' 'Self Build,' to name but a few. He glanced up at the clock, it was 2.45pm. In his world, to be behind 15 minutes, was a crime. He had made the effort to get there early, if only by a few minutes, but early is cool, late is not.

Flicking through his chosen read 'Homes and Gardens,' finally the receptionist called over asking him to go upstairs to room 11.

He stood at the door and knocked a couple of times.

"COME IN!" the voice commanded. He placed a sweaty palm onto the door handle and pulled it down. The squeaky handle opened the door inward. There at a desk across the room, sat a man, about 45, sporting an untidy head of black hair, and a greying goatee beard, reminding him of Billy Connolly.

"Ahh, yes, good afternoon, Bruce, is it?" asked the man.

"Yes, I am he, pleased to meet you Mr Campbell I presume?" The man stood up and reached out his right hand, Bruce stepped over and offered his. Their eyes locked as they shook hands.

"Good to meet you, Bruce, call me Ken, formalities tire me in this job!"

"Great...Ken, it is," said Bruce.

"Please, grab a chair Bruce, let's get to business."

Bruce sat back into a dark polished seat, upright but bragging a comfy button-backed soft leather, matching the desk. The desk had a fancy inlaid jade green leather pattern, beneath a glass top. The office was bright coloured, a combination of light grey and pastel green.

It was indeed a very formal setting. Ken slapped a blue file onto the desk. He pulled a few sheets of paper from within and using an index finger, started to follow the wording.

"Right, I won't beat about the bush Bruce. This is a last will and testament. It was signed and witnessed 11th of July 2006, just on two years ago." He followed a few more lines with his finger, and sat back in his chair, breathing out a lengthy sigh.

"Your aunt, Mrs Alice Dogherty, she seemed to have your interests at heart," he said

A few more tense moments passed by. Bruce clenched his hands together rubbing the clammy perspiration. 'Come on, come on, for God's sake,' he thought.

Ken placed the papers down on the desk and looked at Bruce, before clearing his voice.

"Bruce, I can confirm your aunt has left you a substantial amount of money and property. In fact, I have double read through the particulars and re-checked them all."

Bruce drew in a deep breath and was about to ask him to elaborate. Ken continued further:

"I can confirm you are the single beneficiary; The Dunella Hotel is to be transferred into your name, and you have a lump sum in cash of £125,000. That is net after all fees."

Bruce froze, not quite knowing how to respond. His heartbeat increasing, hands clammier.

"BLOODY HELL!" he yelled.

"Yes, my thoughts too, nice bit of money and a great property," said Ken.

"This is an absolute shock, I'm a bit gob-smacked, a hotel, money, more than I could ever save."

The Dunella Hotel, had been a prosperous business. Aunt Alice struggled on for several years after her husband, Uncle Stanley passed away. It was a difficult decision to make, but she eventually closed the doors and the hotel as a business closed. Much of this was due to her failing health. The building had been extensively refurbished and well maintained. The inheritance money was from a combination of investments made by Stanley, a small life insurance policy and the healthy nature of the business.

"So, what Now?" asked Bruce.

"It's straight forward, I need a few signatures, to enable the release of certain documents, and to gain permission from the estate agent, holding the keys. Thomson property have carried out a preliminary survey."

"And the business, was it doing ok or what?"

Ken opened a top drawer and pulled out a packet of cigarettes. He didn't say much, offering one to Bruce. He declined the offer. Ken struck a match and lit the cigarette, drawing in a deep breath, before exhaling its acrid odour.

"The business was going well, and the bulk of your cash inheritance has come from it. I can say that your aunty got into a spot of bother with some guests," said Ken.

"What sort of bother?"

"Let's just say that certain folk may have been unwilling to stay over at times and were certainly a little sceptical about going back," he added.

Bruce fell silent, wondering what to ask next. He re-called the conversation with the neighbour who bought the settee. He mentioned that not only his aunt but also his mother started to dabble in the spirit world. A shiver shot up and down his back. Was there any truth to the story? The only sure way to find out would be in the hotel. What secrets does the Dunella hotel hold?

"May I ask why?" asked Bruce.

"I'll be honest with you, I only know that things may have gone 'bump-in-the-night' having a bit of an impact on stay overs," said Ken.

"Do you mean its haunted?"

Ken shifted his seat position and looked down at the desk. He looked at Bruce and his frown disappeared. He stared deeply at him, not a single emotion on his face and said: "There are sometimes things going on in this world, that we should leave alone. Some of those things are not always pleasant, and many we can't ever easily understand."

"You haven't answered the question, Ken."

"Look, I'm only going with what some local hear-say has spread around the town. I'm sure it's nothing, your aunt was tired and winding down, her illness not helping her with the stresses of running a large hotel."

"So, when can I officially take ownership and visit Dunella?" asked Bruce.

"Oh, that's easy, did you not just sign the paperwork?"

"Yes, I did."

"Well then, it's up to you to collect the keys from the agent, and she's all yours."

Ken handed him a business card with the estate agent details, before shaking hands.

He made his way to the office door, before turning to ask: "Just one thing, the money bit, is that soon too?" he asked.

"It will take a little over two weeks, due to money laundering formalities and transfer checks. You'll get a further letter soon, fill in your account details, return it to the address and you'll have the money in about ten working days once they receive it back." Bruce left the office and kept breaking into a smile, more of a grin, chuckling like a mad man. The past hour or so had effectively changed his future forever.

# Chapter three

He drove home excited about the news. It's not every day you discover that you own a hotel and have a life-changing pot of money for free. He sat at the kitchen table, briefly peering up at the clock. In what had been just a couple hours, it seemed like hours and hours had passed by. He didn't want to push it with work, but he realised that this opportunity could be a real spring- board to early retirement from the army. He looked at his hands and could see an unusual shaking on the left one. He had given up smoking but had a sudden urge to light one up. Luckily for him there was a half pack of Marlborough Lites in the bottom of a kitchen drawer. He reached into the drawer, rummaging through piles of old letters, mixed up with useless kitchen utensils and semi spent batteries. He eagerly grabbed the packet. Lifting the lid, finding three full cigarettes. They had sat there, un-touched for almost a year since he kicked the habit.

    Nicotine had always been a good friend for Bruce. Being a witness to some of the world's worst war-torn countries, there was nothing better than to light up in times of stress. He had kicked the habit due to feeling breathless while out jogging. He had a check-up at the med centre on base. All was well and he passed all the tests, but the doc suggested he should quit smoking, so he reluctantly did so. Today, was unusual, he had difficulty processing everything. He lit the cigarette on the gas hob and threw the back door open. Standing there, like you would do visiting a mate's house, he drew in a long drag. He tried not to cough, but it was inevitable. He tried another and this time it wasn't so bad. Eventually the whole cigarette was gone, just a butt left. He felt a bit better, still reeling from the thought that he had a huge inheritance. Not just a super hotel, but a life-changing sum of money to go with it. Another hour passed by. He was still messing around with things he wouldn't normally bother with. He wasn't usually interested in DIY, but he found himself tinkering with a wonky kitchen drawer. The time had come; he picked up the telephone and dialled the agent's number.

"Good afternoon, Thompsons, how may I help you?" the pleasant female voice asked.
He clears his throat, searching for his most masculine of responses.

"Yes, hi, erm, hello, I am Bruce... Bruce Gordon, I need to talk to someone about visiting Dunella Hotel please?" he asked.

"Yes, I have been expecting a call from you, Mr Gordon. I have your survey results and the keys to sign for," she said.

"Brilliant, when can we meet for a viewing." He was trying not to sound too keen, his hands starting to clam up again.

"Right, hold one sec, checking the diary, it's not me who will meet you, I'm just the receptionist." The line went quiet as she sifted through the diary.

"Yes, my colleague Cindy Campbell, she has a slot on Monday 9th or actually this Saturday morning if you're available?"

"Tomorrow, that's sudden," he replied.

"My father used to say, 'strike whilst the iron's hot,' Mr Gordon. Are you available then?"

"I am indeed free, that suits me. No golfing planned this weekend," he joked.

The receptionist made the appointment for 10am. He felt relieved that this was happening almost straight away. They talked about the address and things to expect at the viewing. Bruce knew the hotel, having stayed as a youngster briefly. Before he had ever any thought to join the army, his parents booked a single night there, when they attended a friend's wedding close-by.

He was just twelve years old, when his father booked two rooms, one for himself, the other a twin for just Bruce and his mother. The rooms were joined by a double door, so they were not completely segregated. There was little to do that night. Back then, you were lucky to get a television let alone a colour one. His dad kicked his black shiny shoes off and lay on his double bed. It was a Friday evening; the wedding was the following day. It had long been a favourite hotel in Broughty Ferry, for friends and family to check in, usually the night before the main event. It had been a local myth for years, that it was lucky to check in for a wedding. There was probably little truth in it. His father soon dosed off, while his mother turned on the old TV.

It was 1972, most TVs were black and white in the U.K, but the hotel had American imports that were colour. Back then there were just three channels to choose from, BBC 1, BBC 2 and ITV. Sheila pushed the buttons in and out, turning each knob as she went. Finally finding an episode of The Waltons.

She put the tiny kettle on and rummaged through the thin selection of tea and coffee. She made an unknown brand of coffee, and Bruce was lucky enough to get a hot chocolate. Alec was already asleep, his snoring passing through from his adjoining room. Eventually, the Waltons ended, and they got into their single beds. Sheila turned out the little bedside lamp on a table between them. It was now pretty much pitch black. The only light passing into the window, from the cars passing by on the main road outside. It wasn't long before Sheila started her own snoring. Bruce lay there, wide awake, listening to the uncomforting melody of his parents snoring.

He prayed that he would fall asleep, but just lay there, still, trying to warm up in the chilly bed.

At one point, he heard odd noises, a sort of rattling and the occasional thump. As it was an old building, even a 12-year-old boy wouldn't think too much of it. However, that night the noises seemed to go on endlessly. Bruce stared at the ceiling, praying for sleep to come, his ears still being assaulted with the snoring from his parents. He turned over to the right, looking over at the door separating the rooms. At one point, it appeared to move, slowly closing, silent as it went. His heart starting to pound, not sure if he was dreaming or witnessing something paranormal. There was a window ajar slightly, but the night was not windy, with clear skies.

He felt afraid. He turned to the opposite side of his bed, hoping that his mother would wake. She didn't, but her arm had fallen out of the bed. He reached out to grab her hand, longing for instant relief and comfort from his night demons. He grabbed the hand. Suddenly, and totally unexpected, she woke, snatching her hand away screaming, and sat up: "WHAT THE FLYING SHIT BOLLOCKS WAS THAT?" she cried out, searching for the table lamp. Bruce fell silent, retracting away slightly.

"WHAT'S GOING ON IN THERE?" Alec shouted from the other room. The table light went on, illuminating the darkness, bringing the relief Bruce was yearning for.

Sheila jumped out of the bed at that point, looking down between the two beds. Her breathing increasing as she was clearly startled. Alec's snoring returned as he had quickly gone back to sleep. "Something touched my hand; it scared the crap out of me Bruce," she said, clutching her chin and pointing at the bed. He did not know what to say, knowing it was him who touched her, in the dead of the night. Sheila was now in a state of shock; she sat down on the small chair in the corner and lit up a cigarette. She looked over at Bruce, who was sitting up in bed.

"Darling, that was terrifying, I didn't mean to frighten you."

"It's fine mum, maybe you had a bad dream!" he replied,

She sucked in another deep drag on the cigarette, the smoke slowly filling the room.

"Honestly Bruce, that was creepy, trust your dad to book a haunted room."

Bruce knew that he was the 'ghost' and wondered if he should own up. He decided not to, instead offering his mum a comforting voice.

"It's fine mum, you had a bad dream, it happens, there's no such thing as ghosts."

Eventually that night, she settled down and got to sleep. The beauty of the whole incident was that she left the bed-side table lamp on.

That was the only memory he had of Dunella, a creepy one at that. Knowing that he had terrified his mother at the time, often brought a smile to his face. Tomorrow, he would be back there once again, on a very different basis this time.

It was the next morning. He woke early, at 6am. He didn't sleep well, due to the anticipation of the morning ahead. He was very used to waking early and never had to set an alarm. With just three hours until the viewing, he had to make his early morning jog a quick one. He threw on his running gear and headed off out. It had rained during the night, and the ground was wet. The sky was now clear, but there was a chilly breeze. He started off along a track, just opposite his home. The pathway ran to the side of a farmer's field. He would normally run about a mile out, sometimes two, giving him a decent run distance of two or four miles. Today, he chose just two. The pathway was fairly narrow, just enough to allow two people to pass side by side. It was used as a dog-walkers route mainly, and kids taking a short-cut to the local secondary school. There were bushes all along the left-hand side, with multiple trees, sometimes used by idiots drinking and using drugs. The way ahead was soggy, the ground beneath his feet mulchy and slippery here and there.

Bruce always found a good morning run a perfect way to relax. That seems an unusual statement, relax whilst running. It has been proven for many years that certain endorphins are released during exercise. So, although your body is going through its paces, and your heartbeat is raised, the brain falls into a state of relaxation. In fact, doctors now recommend exercise as a good way to reduce stress and in worse cases, depression. It was working well for Bruce. The run gave him time to think about the past couple of days. He had not really thought about the impact a small fortune would have on his life, and certainly what to do with a hotel. The options were numerous. The main one was, that he could now retire from his desk job a couple of years earlier than planned.

Off into the distance at the turning point he had in mind, he could see his next-door neighbour, approaching rapidly. Jimmey Cartwell, a nice guy, similarly aged, but all the same, a nosey parker. He lived alone; his only hobby was walking the dog. That morning, he was out walking Loki, a beastly German Shepherd.

"Hey Bruce, all good?" he asked.

Bruce slowed to a stop and placed his hands on his hips, breathing in deeply. He exhaled a long breath of steam, chilled by the cool morning temperature.

"Hey Jimmey, yeah all is fine with me, yourself?"

He pulled on the lead, making sure Loki wasn't in pounce mode.

"I'm really good ta, see your still keeping fit?"

"Yes, that's me, as many mornings as I can fit in."

"Right, I've not seen you out on a Saturday this early before, in fact, you're usually a weekday man," said Jimmey.

This is exactly the sort of thing that irritated Bruce. How would Jimmey know what days he goes out for a jog? The cheek of it, the 'nosey' branding vindicated right there. Bruce was determined not to give away anything about his recent business. At the same time, he didn't want to sound rude. Compelled to give an answer, he had to think quickly, to fashion a good enough reason.

"I was just adding in an extra day this week, Jimmey, got a few pounds to lose, no reason other than that."

Jimmey looked directly at him and nodded, not entirely convinced, fishing for more.

"I see, right yes, I get that. I noticed your car was out for a good bit yesterday, you go anywhere nice?"

Bruce felt his blood start to boil; his neighbour seems to be the perfect candidate for a military interrogator. "Ah yes, I did have a bit of time off, car needed a new exhaust," said Bruce. He wondered why he said that, knowing that Mr nosey would probably inspect it only to see that it's about six years old and tarnished with rust. Another dog-walker approached causing Loki to bark, very loudly, typical of a German Shepherd. Bruce used the moment to make his apologies to leave. He ran a couple of hundred metres ahead, looking out for the old Oak, he used as the turning point, just a mile out from home. He stopped, and looked back along the path, hoping that Jimmey was going homeward and not stood chatting with another dog owner. He waited a few minutes, sucking in the cool morning air, feeling pretty good and certainly filled with excitement about the up-coming viewing.

Confident the coast was clear; he set off home. It was now just after 7.30am, not too much time left to get ready for the appointment at nine. He took a quick shower and put on his favourite pair of denim jeans, and a casual short sleeved shirt. He grabbed a slice of toast and set off for Broughty Ferry. The drive from Leuchars camp, only took about twenty minutes. On the way, Bruce had plenty of thoughts going through his head. He was still coming to terms with the news that the hotel was his. Was it in disrepair? Was it in good order? Could it still be a working hotel? Just a few of the thoughts bombarding his head.

As he got closer, the buildings became much larger and typical of the area. There were a few hotels, scattered about the town, and all looked similar, with Georgian and Victorian styling. Nearly all were built with light grey stonework. He knew exactly where the hotel was. Number 13 Albany Road. Unlucky for some thirteen. Hopefully that number wasn't a bad omen.

He pulled into the circular and very substantial drive. It appeared tidy and well kept, winding around from the main road, past the main entrance and back out. Off to the left was a decent sized car park, enough for 20 or so cars. On the opposite side, a partly screened area, for bins and what looked like a utility shed. The front of Dunella looked magnificent. There were two floors, but the top had a rooftop private quarter. That was a significant addition, built on top of the existing roof, courtesy of Uncle Stanley. This was part terraced, surrounded by ornate pink marble balustrades between a couple of grand conical towers, either side. Parts of the grey stone building were covered in thick Ivy.

He parked just to the left of the entrance; it was 8.55am. There were no other cars in the driveway, and he assumed that the agent was late. He switched off the engine and sat looking at the entrance. There were a couple of fancy looking timber doors, with the bottom half solid and the top glazed, with a large golden 'WELCOME,' etched into the glass. At each side of the entrance were impressive looking columns, a pink marble, both very shiny. He looked around the area, absorbing the atmosphere. The overall look of Dunella was a bit creepy. Of course, at the moment it was empty of anyone, and an empty car park is always a little strange. It was perhaps an ominous sign, that the heavens opened and suddenly a downpour came.

Suddenly, out of nowhere, a knock on the driver's side window. It was a young woman, with long dark hair, holding what looked like a dark file on her head, trying to shelter from the rain. He assumed it must be the agent and wound down the window, just a few inches so as not to get the car soaked.

"Mr Gordon?" said the woman.
"Yes, that's me, and you are?"
"I'm Cindy...Cindy Campbell, from Thompsons, let's go inside, it's getting heavier."

Just as she uttered those words, there was a clap of thunder. The rain pouring, he knew he was going to have to make a dash for it. Cindy wasted no time at all and scurried across the driveway to the entrance porch. He jumped out of the car, not bothering to lock it up and followed at pace. He got to the first of three stone steps, trying not to slip on them.

Cindy stopped short of the double doors, turning to reveal a semi-soaked head of hair, frantically brushing the rain off her skimpy office attire. She was a pretty woman, late 20's and very slim. She had shoulder length dark brown hair. Her business suit was dark blue and accented with a white blouse. Bruce held out his hand to shake hers, and she did so. They locked eyes for a moment, Bruce was immediately attracted to her, trying not to make it too obvious. After all, he was a man approaching 50.

"Apologies I was a bit late Mr Gordon; I got side-tracked at the office, was about to leave and the postman arrived with a ton of mail."

"No problem at all, Cindy, call me Bruce, Mr Gordon is way too formal for me."

She put a hand into a small shoulder bag, rummaging around: "Here, we go, the keys," she said, dangling a bunch with several keys on it. She proceeded to unlock the double doors, immediately dashing over to reset the alarm as the bleeping sound was a countdown to setting off the alarm. She punched in a code and closed the panel door. The alarm was deactivated. Bruce followed her in and closed the door behind him. The entrance lobby was a large space, with a soft two-seater sofa on each side, above each one, cork notice boards with a plethora of out-dated leaflets and taxi business cards pinned onto them. He was immediately struck with the musty smell; causing him to sneeze a couple of times, due to the dust they disturbed when they walked in. The stormy weather had reduced the inside of the lobby to a dull gloom, adding to its slightly foreboding feeling. Cindy walked into the reception area. She placed her file onto a small Oak table at the bottom of a long mirror. She opened a small cupboard door that was already slightly ajar and popped a cover open inside. With a flick of a switch, she turned on the electricity.

Bruce stood in the reception, gazing straight ahead at the most incredible looking grand staircase. Just off to the right was the reception check-in area. The reception area remained gloomy whilst she went to the back area of the reception and opened another door. Bruce, still taking in the view of his inheritance, shivered due to the cold, shrugging off a chill that ran up and down his spine.

"There we go, just these too," she said. Eventually she found the switch bank in the manager's office. She flicked a few more on, and the reception lighting lit above the check-in desk. The grand staircase lit up as did the entrance porch area.

"Way better," said Bruce.

"Yes, but its freezing, I guess the boilers are shut off at the moment," she replied.

She carried on fumbling around the back area of the reception desk. Bruce had a chance to walk around the large lobby. It appeared that the hotel had just seized to stop working. Everything was ready-to-go. It was as if the place had been momentarily frozen in time. The thing that stood out the most for Bruce, was the deathly silence. No human traffic, no porters, no chitter chatter, telephones ringing or the clunking of crockery; the usual things associated with a busy hotel.

He noted a few beautiful paintings on the wall. These were large and there were a few of them. Most seemed to depict Broughty at the turn of the century. There was one between two doors. It was a blown-up poster photograph of Dunella, circa 1920. There was an old car, like a model T Ford in the drive, a couple of maids dressed in white stood in the entrance and what looked like a gardener wheeling a barrow towards an archway. A moment caught in time forever, now hanging between the gents and the ladies' toilets.

He pushed the gent's door open, before entering inside. The lights were also on, as he pushed open the inner door. He was immediately struck with a strong smell of sewage. The initial shock causing him to wretch slightly. He walked over to a window and opened it, momentarily struggling with a stiff brass window catch. The window was stuck. He gave it a thud with a clenched fist, and it opened, allowing a gust of a welcome breeze to flood in. He turned to view the toilet as a whole. There were four cubicles, a long bank of urinals, four in total including the lower down version for younger children, or in-fact little people, commonly known as dwarfs.

The suite was dark reddish in colour, a kind of stained mahogany. The sinks, four in all were a white ornate Victoriana style with fancy gold plated taps. These had the typical plunge plug in the centres. The mirrors were full length, rising from the top of the vanity unit to the ceiling. He noted the right-hand end was cracked. He took the opportunity to take a pee in one of the urinals. The smell was not particularly pleasant, as the water to the hotel was still turned off. He tried to flush but the handle just swung loose.

"BRUCE," a voice called out. He had little to no time to reply. "BRUCE," the voice called out once again.

He quickly shook off the remnants off a forced pee and replied in kind: "BE THERE IN A MOMENT!"

Finished, he reached to the nearest tap and twisted it on; it screeched open but only a drop or two came out. "Bloody hell," he said, forced to wipe his hands down the sides of his jeans.

He left the toilet to find Cindy looking slightly startled. "There you are Bruce, thought I'd lost you already," she said.

"No not yet, I was trying out the gents. If you need the ladies, be warned, the waters still off!"

"It won't be off too long, there's a handyman that comes in twice weekly, just to keep check on things. I'll make a note for him to get it turned back on." She opened her file and pulled a few sheets of paper out. She spread them over the reception desk.

"There we are Bruce, this is a plan of the basement, the 1'st, 2n'd and top floors too."

He peered over the plans, of which he had never seen anything quite like it. He had never been involved in a building project and wasn't particularly handy when it came to DIY.

"Great, but where's the lift? he asks.

"That's along the corridor along on the left there. The kitchens are at the end of the same corridor.

She threw her long hair back and walked over to the bottom of the stairs. "This place is magnificent, so grand and atmospheric; you must be over the moon Bruce."

He turned from the papers and looked her squarely in the eye. "It's a bit of a shock, I'll be honest. Until this all came about, I was just plotting my retirement from the army."

"Oh, a soldier? they didn't say, I love a good war story," she said.

He was full of real war stories, but typical of a career soldier, he never really talked about the business of killing. It wasn't always about killing though. He had been on humanitarian missions, and involved in missions within the U.K. The brutal part of soldiering is the taking of life, but put into a percentage, that parts usually about five percent of a soldier's job. The bulk of soldiering is taken up with training, and camp duties. In fact, soldiering can at times be a boring role. Someone once said to Bruce, that the army is like a 'shaken bottle of coke.' Once shaken, it just sits there, inanimate, but ready, until the lid is taken off, then all hell breaks out.

Cindy walked through the reception area to a set of part glazed double doors, to the right of the grand staircase. There was a large etching sign across the two upper glass panels:

**'CULLODEN ROOM.'**

She fiddled with a padlock on a chain.

"Blast it, why is this room locked?" she said. She tugged on the lock again, but nothing budged.

Bruce stepped over and grabbed the lock. He struggled with it too, while Cindy went back to reception and rummaged around at the back of the check-in desk. "Here we are, a nice envelope full of keys," she said. At that moment, there was a loud knock on the entrance door. Bruce looked around to see the figure of a man staring through the window. He walked over to the inner door and went through to the entrance lobby. The man had a hand up at the glass, waving in a circular motion, leaving marks from his breath. Bruce opened the door. There, stood an older looking man, appearing weathered, late fifties or early sixties. His grey thick head of hair looked damp from the wet weather. He was wearing dark work trousers, the type with pockets on either side, spattered in paint. His top was similarly messy. His black fleece was spattered in all colours. What stood out the most, was a facial scar, that ran from chin across his face to his right ear. The door opened.

"Hello, um, I'm." he said. Then he was rudely interrupted from a voice inside: "ARCHIE!" called Cindy.

He looked past Bruce and smiled as she walked over, clutching the key filled envelope.

"I forgot you were coming, just in time, we need a set of keys," she said.

Bruce stepped aside to let him pass, noting that he smelled like a carpenter's workshop, a mix of glue and sawdust.

"I have all the keys you need, we had arranged for me to come, remember?" he said.

He had a broad Scots accent, a raspy voice, fitting of a man who works in dusty environments.

"I had forgotten you were coming to be honest; the weather was a bit of a distraction. You turned up at the right time," said Cindy.

"I always aim to please, I've been here so long now, I never let Dunella down," he said proudly

He reached out to Bruce, not knowing who he was and took his right hand, gripping it tightly and said: "You must be the new owner?"

"Yes, I'm Bruce, and what do you do here?" he asked.

"I'm the handyman, been here on and off since the early 90s now, there's little I don't know about this place."

"We could use a few doors being unlocked, the Culloden, its padlocked, are there anymore locked up?" asked Cindy.

"I think there's a few upstairs, a couple of out buildings, and room 19; that's definitely locked," he said, his accent causing them to virtually lip-read. He took out a large bunch of keys from his fleece and felt around for the right key. He went over to the Culloden double doors and tried the lock. It clunked open. "There you go, all yours, ye twa. I'll be aroond the place, opening up. Take care in there." He headed upstairs, the treads creaking as he went.

Cindy entered Culloden first, Bruce followed closely. The room was already lit up; the lights probably went on when Cindy flicked the switches at reception. They were inside the heart of Dunella. This was the function suite, used for everything from weddings, business seminars, exhibitions and funeral wakes. The room was more like a hall, with a high up ceiling, part timber panelling on the walls, a long bar along the right-hand side. The size was a surprise, like a small theatre with a functional stage at the far end. There was a gorgeous stone-built fireplace that took up much of the wall on the left-hand side. It had a long, grey coloured granite mantel piece. Bruce noticed a large circular mirrored lamp in the middle of the ceiling, a disco ball as they are commonly known. The walls above the dark brown, varnished panelling, were a warm cream colour. The whole atmosphere in the room was inviting and everything seemed in good order, with a strong smell of fresh paint. In fact, there were a few tins of paint here and there and a pair of two of steps. Part of the bar was covered in light brown cloth dust sheets.

"What's the strong paint smell?" he asked.

"Oh, that's Archie's handiwork, he's been maintaining the place, he's a jack-of-all trades, you're lucky to have him." She paced around the room, feeling the panels and taking a good look around. Bruce was intrigued by the stage; it was like a real theatrical one. There were two bright red curtains at each side, reaching from the timber floor almost to the ceiling. Complete with a full complement of stage lighting above, with all manner of coloured lenses, pointing down at the floor. Bruce wanted to investigate further and walked over to the stage. At the front, was a set of four wooden steps.

He started to climb up and reaching the stage platform, turned to look back across the room.

He threw his arms out and shouted out to Cindy: "THIS IS MAGNIFICENT!"

Startled by his sudden outburst, she replied in kind. "It certainly is that, Bruce. You'll have to brush up on your singing." He did a twirl and as he did, the stage floor creaked loudly.

"Archie said be careful Bruce, maybe the stage is unsafe," said Cindy.

He took her advice and slowed his enthusiasm.

There were several tables scattered around, in no particular order. Cindy pulled a couple of chairs from under one and sat down. She had the envelope full of plans and spread them on the table. He joined her, taking a welcome seat.

"This place seems to be in great order," said Bruce.

"It really is, you know it's practically ready to go live again."

"Live, as in start trading?"

"Well, yes, it's in fine order, much of which you owe to a certain caretaker."

"Yes, of course, he seems to be part of the fixtures and fittings, pardon the pun."

"All I know is, that he knew your late Uncle Stanley, back when it first got re-furbished. He was close to your aunty too, and he's been fixing this place up for some 30 years."

Uncle Stanley had given work to Archie, not long after the hotel was completed, just after the refurb in the late 80's. The hotel had been operating very well, but a few months in, due to the age of the building, and an on-going issue with plumbing, namely bad drainage, a small advert was put in the local paper. Stanley was in his late 60s at this point and he didn't have the time or energy to under-take all the maintenance tasks that were mounting up.

Back then, that was the 'done' thing. Nowadays, it's common to upload jobs online. Back in the early 90s, it was still very common practice to put an advert in a paper and a shop window.

A few days had passed by. Stanley was giving up hope, especially after one morning. A guest from the first floor had come running to reception. It was 7am on a Sunday morning. The guest was woken up by a gargling noise, perpetuating a foul smell.

The toilet was blocked. With no on-site caretaker or handyman, Stanley grabbed his bucket and plunger, pulled on his marigold gloves and attended the room. He could see why the smell had been the issue. There in front of him, trailing out of the bathroom, like a flow of evil coloured lava, was a pool of raw sewage. He looked beyond that sight to the toilet and could see the bubbling and heard the burbling noises. In a panic, he grabbed the towels from the heated rail and threw them down, praying that they would absorb the mess. The flow didn't stop, bubbling up and over the toilet rim. Not really thinking, and maybe from experience that sometimes helped, he flushed the toilet. This could go one way or the other. The fresh water immediately overflowed, onto the mass of towels, but then with a frothy gurgling whoosh, the weight of water with the help of gravity, cleared the toilet. This was typical of Dunella. The upsetting bit was that the guest demanded a refund, quite loudly at reception, almost spitting at the young receptionist. In the end, they were offered a free meal that evening, they accepted.

Fortunately, that afternoon, as if by divine intervention, the receptionist took a call. It was a young man, in his mid 20s, by the name of Archie.

Bruce was sat a little uncomfortably in a chair that seemed to have a wobble. He wondered how competent his inherited caretaker was. Cindy was still sifting through some of the plan pages, deciding where to take the viewing. They could hear walking upstairs, footsteps, assuming that it was Archie, they ignored it. Suddenly, the double doors swung open, it was the man himself.

"There you both are, all opened, ready to go, all yours," he said

"Great. thanks a lot for your time this morning, are you leaving the keys?" she asked.

"No need, you just need to worry aboot setting the alarm, that's it."

Bruce was still looking up at the ceiling, he could swear the footsteps were going on at the precise moment Archie made himself known.

"Archie were you above here a minute ago?" asked Bruce.

Archie cleared his throat and looked up at the ceiling. "Errm, not me, I was at the other end of the corridor and used the fire escape stairwell. Whys that?"

"Oh, nothing, creaking from wind I imagine, was good to meet you by the way, when are you back here?"

"I am here just two days a week at the moment, just for a few hours each day. My next jolly is on Wednesday; I'll be completing this room."

Bruce discounted the unidentified sound above them and stood up to see Archie at the doorway.

"I am going to need a hand around here, if you're interested in a bit of overtime?" said Bruce.

Archie looked over his shoulder and seemed to be more interested in looking at his watch, as if to suggest he was late for something.

"Bruce, I'll give that a thought, I could use the extra pay at the moment, thanks for the offer."

"Righteo, I need to dash, goodbye Cindy, Bruce, be good now."

With that, he closed the doors and left.

"Right, we should get on, I have one more appointment this afternoon. There is a basement, two floors above us, a kitchen, oh and a small matter of 36 rooms," she said, confident she had the right information from the plans.

"Incredible, all mine too, I don't know where to start to be honest Cindy. Archie...is he paid?"

"As far as I'm aware, he is not. He is volunteering to look after the place."

"Well, that's not fair on him at all, I'll be changing that if he comes on board with this project," said Bruce.

"He has been serving this place for a good while, I guess it all means something to him," he added.

Archie had been paid, and very well when he was under Stanley. He eventually started working 40 hours plus per week. After Stanley passed away, Alice tightened the belt on investment quite a bit. The impact was that Archie lost 16 hours per week, effectively becoming part-time. That suited him because he himself had inherited his home from his mother. With no debts, rent or mortgage to worry about, he was happy coming into Dunella for three days a week. Occasionally, Alice would ask him in to perform emergency tasks, bumping his money up quite a bit.

After Alice passed away, that was the end of pay. The hotel had stopped trading just a few months before her death. She had been ill for some time with an asbestos related illness, causing lung cancer.

During her illness, that lasted for a little over two years, she started to wind down the business. It was a shock to her friends and colleagues that she had an asbestos related illness. Traditionally, it was men who were affected. Stanley was more than likely a candidate for being exposed to its evil fibres. Sometimes though, it can catch you if you are walking through an area where it has been exposed. When the initial re-furbishment was going on, it was very likely that materials made from it had been used or disturbed. This is how Alice may have caught a fibre or two. It can enter the lungs, embedding itself in the tissue. The nature of a fibre is like a barbed arrow. It will lodge itself into lung tissue, tiny, not even causing a sneeze. As the years pass by, white blood cells try to attack it and break it down. This fails due to the hardy structure. Eventually, the cells themselves multiply in the area, causing tumours to grow.

There were no children to take over the running of the place. The costs to run the hotel were on the up. This coincided with competition locally, drawing guests away to a more modern equivalent. There was a good amount of money in the bank from prosperous years, but she found herself eating into that, to shore up costs. Alice never wanted to sell the hotel, but gradually she was forced to lay off staff and soon the hotel was left empty. She had made sure that any debts were settled, and that the business was in good hands, should it be revived. Her thoughts turned to her only nephew, Bruce. Aware that due to her rapidly failing health she needed to set a will in place, he was the only obvious candidate.

Meanwhile, Cindy placed the plans away carefully, handing them to Bruce.

They decided to head upstairs to explore the first floor.

On the way up, Bruce noted that the stairwell was covered in lots of paintings. Some were recent and almost new looking. Others were older, more antique in nature. A particular one stood out. It was Claypotts castle from not too far away. The castle, a ruin now, is often chosen by budding artists who love painting or drawing old ruins. This one was different in the sense that someone had drawn it, but they had managed to create an image of the castle long before its current state. That time would have been during the Anglo-Scottish wars. In fact, upon further inspection there was a small brass plaque stating:

***Claypotts Castle as seen after the completion by John Strachan circa 1668***

He remembered as a child, a story his father told him. To this day, Bruce feels a shiver down his spine at the thought of the 'Green Lady,' who has been seen numerous times over the past few centuries. Soldiers and security guards have often reported an eerie feeling, just before the temperature drops. There's often a sudden stillness observed just before a shimmering green light is seen. This light, often takes the form of a human and due to the shimmering shape, appearing with an old-fashioned style dress. The sightings have been attributed to a female.

They were on the first-floor landing. To the left, was a long corridor, mirrored by another to the right. Both were already lit up, thanks to Archie. There were a few rooms on the ground floor, adjacent to the kitchens, still not explored. The room number on the left side corridor started at 107, with doors along one side only.

"Bruce, there are six ground floor rooms. This is the next in sequence," said Cindy.

"I figured that we missed the ground floor ones," he replied.

"Not missed, just left for now, I thought I'd give you a brief tour of each floor for the time-being as I'm a little pushed for time." They walked further along the corridor. The theme was similar to Culloden room. Darker varnished panels below a cream-coloured wall. There were small, brass lamps dotted along each side of the corridor, creating a welcome feeling. Between each room door, was another historical type of painting. One particular one was of Jedburgh Abbey, a ruin established in approximately 1100ad. The carpet, similar to the reception area, a mix of dark blue with gold spots and stars. Cindy led the way, stopping about halfway along the corridor. The lamp outside the door was flickering. On the dark stained door, was a brass number. It was room number 110.

"There we are, halfway along, there's eight rooms in each corridor," she said, confident she had read the plans correctly.

She pulled down on the brass handle, opening the door. Reaching inside, she felt for a switch, finding several, she switched them all on. She opened it fully and went inside, Bruce followed closely. She rushed over to the window, clambering around the nets, looking for a handle. "God almighty, this rooms pretty rank," she said.

"I have to agree, what's that stink," replied Bruce.

"It's just how they go after weeks of inactivity, the wastes and drains are not flushing through enough." The room was pleasantly decorated. This time the theme was less woody and less cream. The walls were a simple painted magnolia, with a white dado rail running around each one. The ceilings were lower, with circular down-lighting, quite modern in appearance.

The furniture, comprising of a typical pine wardrobe, double bed, chest of drawers and a side unit, with a kettle and selection of coffee and tea on a brass stand. All of this, finished off with dark blue carpet and matching curtains. Nestling in the right-hand corner adjacent to the entrance, was the bathroom. Bruce looked inside, the door ajar, he just pushed a little and it swung open, releasing more of the stagnant smell.

He reached for a pull-chord in the dark and pulled down on it.

"Oh, my Lord, I think these rooms and loo's need a good clean and freshen up," he said.

Cindy had located a window handle and swung the window outward.

"Yes, that goes without saying Bruce. If you want this place to re-open as a functioning hotel, you need to consider all these things,"

He looked around the bathroom, noting a tear in a white, stained shower curtain. The suite was a bit dated looking, all white chip board units, white tiles and a black and white diamond shaped vinyl floor. "These rooms are they all like this?" he asked.

"Yes, more or less, apart from the 2$^{nd}$ floor, there's a couple of grand rooms, bridal suites, oh and the private living quarters."

"I see, considering the grand building and the history of this place, they are very modern and contemporary," he said.

"Yes Bruce, dare I say it, like a typical Premiere inn. This is what the market demands, modern, basic luxury."

"I'm not seeing too much in the way of luxury, basic, yes. Where's the telly and the telephone?"

"They are all gone, removed when it shut down, all out of date, not worth anything. That could be your first expensive overhead. Only hooks in the walls, guess all the pictures are gone too," she said.

Bruce was doing the maths, one of his weaknesses. The thought of the cost of 30 or 40 TV's and telephones entered his head. Not having a clue about such costs, he realised that this wasn't going to be cheap, and he would have to keep track of costs. Suddenly, and with little warning, the wind picked up outside, the through draft caused the door to the room to slam closed. Cindy pulled the window shut. "Oh dear, that wasn't good, bloody wind got up there," she said.

Bruce yanked on the wardrobe handle, and it was hanging on with one screw. Inside was a stale smell, several hangers and a few shelves to one side. He thought about how similar they were to the ones on camp. At least the door had a mirror, not cracked for a change.

Cindy popped into the bathroom. She adjusted her hair in the vanity mirror and pulled on the chord, turning the light off. "I think we need to get going now, I'll take you up to show you another. Might be best if we go up to the bridals."

She pulled on the handle and tugged, but the door remained stuck. She tried again, but it was stuck fast. Bruce closed the wardrobe door and gave it a go. He also pulled, worried about ripping the brass handle off. It was stuck fast. "What the?" he said.

"Must have been the wind- when it slammed," said Cindy. Bruce, not having the best DIY knowledge, watched again as Cindy pulled hard on the handle. She gave up and walked back into the room, He followed. She sat on the end of the bed, Bruce opened a drawer, as if looking for a useful item to open it with. Suddenly, with a creak, the door opened. They both looked around at the door, as it moved slowly inward. They were gob smacked. They looked at each other. Cindy jumped up and froze to the spot. "Well, that wasn't creepy as hell," said Bruce.

He went over to the door, inspecting the handle He saw nothing unusual. He checked around the frame and the door keep. There was nothing odd or out of place. Cindy wanted to see for herself.

"I guess your caretaker is going to be a busy man here, Bruce."

She shrugged it off as a latch requiring an oil. Bruce wasn't so easily calmed. That freaked him out. In fact, he thought, that was the stuff of nightmares, but didn't say anything, not wanting to appear afraid, in front of a young woman. They left the room, making sure the lights were off. The door closed as if nothing was wrong at all. The latch clicked into place quite normally.

They walked to the end of the corridor and through a doorway to a second staircase. This was the back stairs fire escape. The stairwell was clinical, a bit gloomy with shiny steps. Much like the type you see in an old hospital. They climbed the steps up to the second floor.

This time they took the right hand of two corridors. The lighting up here had seen better days. In contrast to the first floor, this one was gloomy. Bruce was trying to contain his emotions. The spooky encounter downstairs was fresh in mind. He admired his young guide, wondering why she was so strong- minded. He guessed that in her trade, she would be used to such things. As before, she made her way along to the middle of the corridor. Bruce could see that this time, the corridor seemed longer, assuming that these were bridal rooms.

"So, are these rooms the bridal suites?" he asked. Cindy stopped at room number 18.

She struggled with the stiff handle; it was also a bit tricky. "Only four of those in total, this one, room 19, next door and on the opposite corridor, another two," she said, still struggling with the handle. "Shall we try 19 instead?" suggested Bruce. She stared along to room 19. That was the room left locked by Archie. They didn't ask why, and now he was gone. With another nudge on the door handle, the door finally opened. She felt inside for the switches and on they went. They entered the room. As before, she ran over to the window, this time a little further away. It swung open, allowing a much-needed breath of fresh air in, taking away some of the musty smell that seemed to be a theme so far.

The room was much bigger this time. It opened up to be quite a posh surprise, compared to the standard one they had been in. This one was decorated with an expensive looking wallpaper. The design looked like a Scottish tartan, light grey, red and blue in places. There was a 4-poster bed, in the middle of the wall to the right. This was featuring ornately carved posts, with a dark pink canopy draped across the top. The lights were made up of two chandeliers, dangling from a much higher ceiling, causing feint reflections on every wall. The fixtures and fittings were expensive, adding to the feeling of grandeur. This time, the carpets were replaced with what looked like solid oak floorboards, deeply polished and looked smooth as ice. Bruce was amazed.

"Wow, this room is a game changer. Obviously, no expense spared here Cindy."

She had plunged into a button backed single chair, covered in a deep red leather.

"This here is a great example of the wedding suites," she said excitedly, as if she were selling the place.

"Great room to come to after a wedding, bet that beds seen some action."

Realising what he had just said, he made his apologies. She giggled and cleared her throat, agreeing that it must have.

"This is something else, the furnishings, what's the bathroom like this time?" he asked.

"Same spec as the rest of it, you'll see."

He walked over to the far corner of the room. The shape of the bathroom formed a hexagonal shape. Inside, he couldn't believe his eyes. The taps sitting atop a very ornate pale white expensive looking sink, bath and bidet, were gold plated. There was a large bay window looking out over the grounds at the rear. He had not yet seen the rear of the hotel. There were extensive gardens, with what appeared to be a couple of ponds right at the back. He took a good look outside, thinking about the work that it might involve. Some of the pathways and what seemed to be a couple of out buildings seemed a bit shabby, with overgrowth everywhere. He lifted the toilet seat, just to see what was going on. Just like downstairs, the water inside was a dirty colour, and had an odour best left undescribed.

The door pushed open: "You all good?" asked Cindy.

"Yeah, good, I see there's a huge back garden and all manner of out buildings."

She walked over to peer through the central window, the only one of four that wasn't frosted.

"Oh yes, that's another job to be getting on with Bruce."

"So, I take it Archie's skillset doesn't stretch to gardening?"

"Bits and bobs, he hasn't got the energy or the time, unless of course you do increase his shifts here."

"I would have thought a place this size required a full-time gardener," he said.

"Oh, yes.... the gardener, full time, err, great idea, there was one, she is no longer with us Bruce."

Cindy turned and made her way out of the bathroom. She plunged herself into her comfortable chair of choice again. He followed and grabbed the back of a small chair from underneath the sideboard. He was curious to hear more about the ex-gardener.

"So, should I contact the gardener and offer her a job?"

Cindy crossed her legs and looked a little edgy.

"It's a sad story, I do know it wasn't very pleasant, and sadly she passed away."

"I'm intrigued Cindy, tell me more, if you have time of course."

"Well Bruce, there was one lady, she was here on and off, part time for years. I know it didn't end well; there were a few others came and went afterwards."

Maureen met aunty Alice, by chance, one afternoon at the local market. The market was held every Sunday, in Gray street. Alice would find herself digging around the stalls, mainly looking for good ideas to spruce up Dunella. They had not long finished the refurb, and it was time to pick the curtains, bedding and all the usual paraphernalia. In a hotel with 36 rooms and a function suite, and several other service rooms and areas, the task wasn't that easy. It certainly wasn't cheap either.

After the purchase of Dunella in early 88, the refurb started almost immediately. Just over a year later, the work was done, and she was almost ready for business. They had used a lot of the money left over for the work but not all. This was put aside for fixtures and fittings and the final bits, involving curtains, bedding, towelling etc. The remainder was invested and this formed part of his inheritance. After several trips to the market, and hours spent trawling the yellow pages, the final touches were made, and the hotel was business ready. For those of you wondering what 'yellow pages' means? This was kind of the first internet. You had a physical book; it was bright yellow and filled with thousands of businesses and numbers. If you wanted anything, you didn't have the luxury of clicking on google. You had to turn the pages, pick up the actual telephone and dial a long number.

The only part of the whole project left to do, at Dunella hotel, was to improve the patio areas at the rear. On this particular day, Alice went to a popular stall. It was huge, more like a mini garden centre, taking up three stall widths and was the largest by far. She spent a lot of time, sifting through garden gnomes, bird tables and wooden bench sets. She picked out a few wiry hanging baskets and got talking to the stall holder. That person was Maureen.

# Chapter four

Maureen had always lived in Dundee. She was born into a prosperous family who were involved with the wool industry. Her father had built his business up at the end of World War One, and like many young men who were demobbed from the army, he had to turn his hand to something.

So, he got himself a job at a farm, just outside Dundee, that specialised in rearing sheep. The days were long, often starting at 5am. For a retired soldier of the Great War, this was still a comfortable alternative, compared to the bitter existence in the trenches. After a couple of years being shown how to breed and sheer the wool from the sheep, Malcolm was approached by two of his ex-comrades. They had served together, and fortune would have it that unlike so many young men, they were gifted a safe return home. The proposition was to purchase a few acres of farmland. Then, after setting up a few pens and outbuildings, they would breed sheep for the purpose of the wool industry. In the 1920s land was very cheap, acres selling for just a few pounds. There was an abundance of available farmland due to the number of farmers and farm hands who lost their lives. The local economy had suffered to the point of despair. Poverty then was very unlike poverty today. If you were on the breadline in the 1920s it literally meant queuing in a line and waiting for a loaf of bread to be donated to you. Maureen was an only child. She was brought up on the sheep farm and became very interested in the food growing aspect of farming. She would get involved with her mother, planting seed and growing herbs. These were sold on at local markets and soon they would set up a stall in Gray street.

Eventually, in her teens, Maureen became interested in growing plants and flowers. Her father built two large green houses for her. She wasn't really interested in the profit aspect of growing, but her dad certainly was. She would grow evergreens mainly, consisting of ferns palms and miniature trees. These were perfect for the house and sold well alongside her thyme, rosemary and juniper berries.

Soon, she was able to expand the market stall, into the size it was when Alice bought her bits and bobs from there. The business fluctuated as usual with seasonal produce. Consequently, she turned her hand, with all the farming knowledge at gardening, when the market was closed. She got a great handful of customers in and around Dundee. Then, one day, she saw a notice in a local D I Y stores noticeboard. It was a job advert for a part-time gardener at Dunella.

Maureen thought about applying and put it on hold initially. Some of her customers were very ad-hoc and she never had set hours. This was something she wasn't used to at all.

That day she met Alice buying the baskets, Alice mentioned that she was from Dunella. Maureen asked about the position, and more or less sealed the deal at the stall. It was now 1990. The hotel was complete and ready for business. By this time, Maureen was 61 years old. She was physically fit and the two-day week at Dunella suited her. She would get to work planting shrubs and bulbs, trying to get a decent spread of colour around the gardens. The key for her was to plant seasonal plants and flowers. Her skills and experience were perfect for such an undertaking.

It was a rainy November morning, chilly, with a horrible damp mist on the grounds of Dunella. By now, Maureen had been at the hotel for just under five years. She had been an integral part to improving the grounds. She was involved in everything from weeding pathways, mowing lawns and simply flower arranging in reception. There were numerous weddings and sadly, wakes, where she would meet with and negotiate with clients to arrange orders. Her time was so limited initially, just working two days per week. Soon it became apparent that she would be required an extra day. This was the case in the summer months.

On this fateful day, she would turn her hand to weeding one of two small ponds at the rear of the hotel. The central one in the centre of the driveway was much larger. The two at the rear were often overlooked, as they were underneath overhanging shrubs and a few small trees. They both had a pump and filter system, that kept the waters looking clear and adding a nice sound of trickling water. The smaller fountains of the two ponds were often getting clogged up with fish food, and pond weed. Maureen was now almost 66. After a lifetime of working outdoors, she had started to suffer from arthritis. This is a pretty awful affliction. Usually, it starts off in the toes, fingers, knuckles and can spread to any joint it chooses. It often comes to those who have spent a life outside, heavy lifting, where the joints are more prone to stress. Gardeners are in that category.

Maureen had already talked about retiring. The market stall had slowed down, and she was putting more time in at the hotel. It was very common for women at that time to stop work at 60, but after she had lost Stanley, she wanted to carry on doing what she loved the most.

Like many times before, she pulled on her wellington boots and headed to the rear of the grounds. Just as she had done, time and time again, she stepped into the freezing water. Sifting through the surface weed and avoiding pulling out Lilly pads, she went to work.

The filter on the pond to the left-hand side had been playing up. They tend to get full of slimy green detritus. The pond was clear of weed and the last thing to do was search for the filter. It was usually at the bottom of the pond, sat on top of a rock. It was only about two feet in depth.

Maureen grabbed hold of the filter housing, and it became snagged on some weeds that were growing stubbornly deep down. She tugged a little bit harder this time, and it would be the last action of her life. The filter came loose, but she pulled out a wire, that caused current to flow out and into the water. The electric current shocking its way through her body. For just a few moments, the shock caused her body to freeze. This was followed by a spasm as the fuse in a nearby shed eventually tripped. This was not the end...yet! Her body relaxed, but the sudden release from the current threw her backwards, hitting her head on a stone bird bath at the edge of the pond.

Her skull, now fractured, caused immediate unconsciousness and she slowly slipped under the freezing water. It took just a few minutes for her lungs to fill as she drowned, unaware, the only humane thing about her death was that she was already asleep.

The month of November was always cold, and sub-zero temperatures were the norm. That year, the hotel was almost deserted. There were a few staff working. The usual handful, including a receptionist who was so quiet, she sat filing her nails at the desk. A chef, also so quiet that he made himself oversized meals, just to give himself something to do. There were two housekeepers on site. Both were great at looking busy, a recently married couple from Romania. There were four rooms sold that week. One of the guests, a businessman from Edinburgh, had checked in for a night. He had been selling dog food to local businesses in Dundee and his partner in crime, was a white poodle, named Florence.

The day of Maureen's death had become foggier, and the temperatures plummeted to five below freezing. She spent the rest of the day, semi submerged, alone and undiscovered. She was used to clocking in and leaving at random times so none of the staff were concerned or even had her in mind. The dark came early that evening, and frost settled all over the grounds. As the night wore on, the shallow ponds started to freeze over, and her body wasn't spared from the arctic conditions.

The next morning, Florence was let of her lead and started to sniff her way around the gardens.

It was when she didn't stop barking and her owner, drawn to the melee, made the grim discovery.

The incident was reported to the police at that time. There was a small investigation, but after just one short court hearing, the decision was arrived at that she had dies by accident.

In the early 90s, it was not so popular for companies to be sewed and made libel for such incidences. The local press, The Courier, ran a small article relating to the death, but it went largely un-noticed, and the hotel carried on as usual.

Presently, Bruce was still curious about the so-called incident that Cindy was touching on. He wanted to know more, and he sensed all was not well. He pushed a little harder.

"So, you say she passed away?"

"Yes, the original one, the lady gardener, not sure of her name," said Cindy.

"That's a real pity, do you know how it happened?"

"I'm not sure, I do know it was an unfortunate incident, I honestly can't elaborate."

Bruce couldn't work out if she knew more or not. Aware of the fact that something had happened, he also felt a certain unease that he couldn't fathom out. He also decided to stop pestering Cindy. In time he would get to know Dunella well enough.

The appointment had gone very well. Cindy dropped another small hint that she had another viewing later that day. They closed the door to the room with a view and made their way downstairs. "Right Bruce, it was great getting to know you. I can say that there's plenty more to explore, but our appointment concludes now," she said, putting a few papers in her bag and brushing a little dust off her shoulders. They took a few minutes to turn out the lighting and made their way to the main entrance. Suddenly, from upstairs, a loud crashing noise was heard. It startled both of them enough to immediately turn around; their eyes focused on the staircase.

"What the flying bollocks was that?" said Bruce. They stared at the staircase, not daring to move. Cindy moved closer to him; he could see her already pale face becoming whiter.

"I have no idea; guess it was a window slamming?"

She turned and scurried to the entrance hallway. Bruce followed and he waited while she set the code on the alarm. He glanced back at the stairwell, a bit creeped out, but shrugged it off as a draft. Cindy puled the double inner doors to the entrance lobby closed and they left. She rattled the key hastily into the lock and put it away.

"Well, that was a bit spooky," she said.

"It was nothing, just a draft and a slamming window, like you said Cindy."

The rain had eased up and they hovered for a few more minutes at the entrance.

"So, what happens now?" he asked.

"The viewing is over, you have had your tour, and now it's up to the solicitors to finalise a few bits and bobs."

"Guess I just wait a while now until that's all done?"

"Yes, just a week I imagine at the most, they are usually very quick after these sorts of viewings."

"Sorts of viewings?"

"The type involving inheritance, they are much faster to complete, compared to a normal sale."

With that, they shook hands, and she turned, making her way towards the main driveway entrance. Bruce walked over to his car and called over just as she was about to disappear around the corner. "Oh, just one thing Cindy?"

She turned to face him. "What is it?"

"Room 19, its locked, any idea why?"

"Not a clue, I'm sure Archie is the one to ask; goodbye now, take care."

He opened the car and sat inside. Taking a few minutes just to absorb the viewing. He was excited, relieved, all sorts of emotions entering his head. He switched on the ignition and turned around to reverse out of the parking bay. Upon turning around again, he noticed a pale shadow in a first-floor window, seeming to be looking his way. The eerie sight was human in form, but with no depth or detail, just a pale grey form. He looked up at it for a moment or two, his hairs raising on the back of his neck. He blinked a few times and rubbed his eyes. Upon re-focusing on the sight, he could see that the window was empty, just darkness behind. The figure was gone.

Bruce started the journey home. The viewing had been exciting, and his young host was great at showing him the old hotel. So much was entering his head. There wasn't a specific time and date for the exact ownership to be made properly. There was also the matter of the cash, lots of it.

His military salary was good, and he had little in the way of debt. Living much of his adult life as a single man had helped. He was often away abroad on deployments. This meant that he mustered large bonus payments, for deployments and combined with his salary, he had a large savings account. Another good investment was one or two that he had made in gold and silver.

All of this meant that he could call upon just under 40k. Combining that with his windfall made a nice tidy figure of around £165,000.

If he decided to retire early, he could invest all of his time bringing the hotel back to its former glory. There were still unanswered questions to be asked. Was there a decent living quarters at the hotel? That was a huge factor in all of this. He had spent many years in his two-bed home just a few minutes cycle from camp. This was an army rental, and the monthly payments were always taken directly from his pay. He would have to serve three months' notice to leave. That wasn't an issue. The biggest thing bothering him now, was the decision to go early. If he stayed on until retirement, the hotel would sit dormant. Such a huge undertaking could never be achieved by one man, at weekends. Or could it? While serving his notice period he would be embroiled there anyway and that was going to be inevitable.

Back home, things seemed a bit surreal. It was almost as if the hotel was calling him, subconsciously. His small practical military home suddenly felt drab and confined. With so much still to explore there and the prospect of contributing to its revival, he was becoming more excited. He was also getting more anxious about major decisions that he knew needed to be made. He spent the afternoon, pacing around, feeling unsettled. He wanted to return to the hotel. He knew he could, and he also knew it would be pointless. There was no chance of getting in. He was going to have to be patient for the legal stuff to be completed. As evening came, Bruce raided the fridge for his last two bottles of beer. It was time to sit at the desk and search the internet.

Broadband was improving by 2008, but still not as fast as it is today. However, it was ok on his recent purchase of a PC with Windows Vista. This package was good enough for internet searches. He settled down cracked open a bottle of beer and typed in a search: **Dunella Hotel.**

He started trawling the internet, swigging his beer as he went. The usual old adverts for breaks popped up, linked to weekend break search engines. Further he went, clicking on links. Page after page, nothing of interest or anything that caught his eye. Bruce recalled checking Trip advisor last time he went away on a short break to the Outer Hebrides. These islands were great for keen fishermen and Bruce fished as often as he could. He clicked on the link, starting to browse down to the hotel. There were plenty of reviews, good and bad. The usual references to uncooked sausages, or dirt on a towel. It seemed to be a theme that Dunella was a bit chilly.

"You can't please everyone, old buggers," he said to himself, making a reference to the older guests.

He carried on, clicking and scrolling, looking for anything of significance. Then he noticed one, then another. These two were added within the last two years of business. The theme was similar, a reference to the pleasant grounds and another to the smiling receptionist, trivial non damming stuff. But these two mentioned something else. One stood out in particular:

*'Great staff, good food, bed mattress a bit hard. Bumps in the night kept me awake, got a discount, wee bit creepy!!!'*

The other one:

*'Lovely place, food ok, staff friendly. If you want a good night's sleep here, think twice, not trying to put you off, probably won't return!'*

These caught his attention. He cracked open the second bottle, taking a good swig. The vision at the window just a few hours earlier creeped him out. The next link, Wikipedia. This was a little more interesting, listing dates from the time Dunella was built to when the hotel recently stopped trading. He read deeper still. There was an article relating to a Mr Tobias Mackintosh. The article was a few lines in length. It did state that there was a grim discovery and a suicide in the 40s. Bruce wondered why the information was so vague, but carried on with his search, trying not to overthink that bit of information.

Tobias was a successful businessman based in Edinburgh as many were. The article was vague but gave an outline of the owner prior to his purchase of the hotel.

Tobias had emigrated from The United States in 1937, the pre-war era. Like many entrepreneurs in the 30s, especially in the U.S, he had struggled during the great depression. The Mackintosh family were linked to the auto industry, and they had set up a company that offered 'while you wait' servicing. Tobias and his brother were doing great for several years during the latter part of the 1920s until the great depression of 1929, all but wiped out the auto industry. People who were fortunate to own a car or a truck at that time, suddenly couldn't muster the cash to have them serviced. This was due to mass unemployment. The brothers had been cautious with money and made several investments in property. They brought in a lot of money from rental properties, nothing special, basic apartments that you wouldn't want to live in too long.

Tobias was married and had a daughter. The damage caused by the depression took its toll on the marriage. Eventually they divorced and Madge Mackintosh disappeared with Holly. Tobias turned to alcohol and became more and more reliant on its ability to mask that pain. However, the brothers drew down some of their investments and after selling of a few garages and properties, they focused on the rental market, refurbishing slums, and taking rents. The brothers had been witnessed arguing and a court battle erupted, linked to each of them accusing the other of dishonesty, embezzlement and fraud. In 1936, they decided to sell up. His brother, William disappeared, and local press had raised the spectre of foul play. Tobias was never linked to the disappearance.

It was shortly after this time of uncertainty and rumour that he emigrated to Scotland, with a small fortune. He didn't waste any time and soon made several property investment purchases in and around Edinburgh and Dundee. One of those was Dunella. Like in the states, most of his property was refurbished into usable small apartments. Dunella was something else. It had been a hotel for some decades but by 1937, she had been completely closed down. The building was just a shadow of her former days. Tobias was a great enthusiast when it came to bringing old buildings back to life. After all, that was how he had made much of his money back in the states. Dunella was no exception. Building work started in early 1938 and by spring of the following year, the hotel was almost completely restored. The state of the building inside and out, would remain almost unchanged for the next 39 years, until Stanley and Alice made their purchase.

The first year went very well for Tobias and profits were on the up. When war broke out, the City of Dundee was over-populated with troops from the UK, Canada Poland and American Gi's. At one point every room was booked thanks to Officers checking in due to training exercises in the nearby hills. He employed a typical handful of staff. Almost all apart from one man, were female. The war effort had made sure of a lack of men. Tobias, single for a while was a bit of a flirt with the ladies. He was in his late 50s at this point and had nothing to do with the war effort. He was definitely not eligible for military service due to his high blood pressure and questionable eyesight. Profits were up and he was enjoying the rewards. He would develop a taste for alcohol, good food and women. Tobias was dating one of the kitchen staff ladies, almost half his age. Shirley, a tall attractive woman with blonde hair and gorgeous green eyes. She didn't exactly help. She knew how to tease a man. At a time when 75 percent of men were serving abroad, a hotel full of army officers from the far-flung allied territories was a dream come true for Shirley.

She would earn her own reputation for sneaking off with a young officer, usually on her days off, but not always. Shirley was caught not once but twice, once mid kissing session in the laundry department, the other time, performing a lewd act down in the cellar. This was going on behind the back of her older employer. Tobias would take her on trips to the hills and spend weekends out at Forfar. This town boasted Glamis castle and had a handful of rooms for hire and several bedrooms. It was a grand alternative to a typical hotel. He would treat Shirley to weekend breaks there, and wining, dining and all the usual romance happened between the couple. Tobias, fell deeply in love with her. Shirley did not. Back at Dunella, rumour was rife that Shirley had been seeing a charismatic Canadian officer. Tobias was aware something was going on but couldn't prove it. The officer himself had also fallen head over heels for Shirley. So, for a time the men dated her, and she kept it as quiet as she could. She was loving the sex offered from the younger man and the money and treats from the elder one.

The young man had developed feelings, and he saw Shirley flirting with Tobias. The same thing happened to Tobias, when he suspected she was seeing him. Both men became jealous. The situation went on for several months. That December, the officers had arranged a Christmas party. The staff laid on quite a spread of food and wine. Considering the food rationing, the hotel had plenty of food in storage and Tobias had a bit of a not so legitimate deal with a local brewer. There were thirty or so young men at the party. The women who were present were from the local auxiliary unit or Territorial volunteer's unit. The staff were busy as ever, in and out of the kitchen and serving drink at the bar. Shirley was head waitress that night. Tobias was happy because her Canadian fling had been posted just a couple of weeks earlier to North Africa.

However, not all was well. She was doing her usual thing with the men. Tobias was raging inside. He kept it quiet but was watching closely. That night, he took up a seat in the Culloden room, by the open fire. The main meal was going on there, but the size of the room meant that you could chill out in leather button backed armchairs, by the fire or along the walls on one of the tables adjacent to the main event table. Tobias had been drinking Whiskey. He was getting drunk but had a knack for hiding it. He lit a pipe and settled back into a comfortable chair. Behind him, he could hear the giggles coming from staff and especially from Shirley.

His blood was boiling. Another whiskey downed, the shrill of her laughter penetrating his brain like a knife. The evening was drawing to a close. Tobias had been watching her and one of the officers. He was making eyes all evening, she was flirting. Just before mid-night, Christmas morning, most of the revellers had gone to bed. Shirley was involved with the clear up and during that time she popped over to kiss Tobias and offer him reassurance. Tobias had enough. He knew that the night for Shirley and her admirer was young. He also knew that the officer's room was first floor, number 19. The officers that were still downstairs were just drinking up, getting ready to head off. Most were drunk. Shirley was still at it. Her admirer seemingly all over her. Tobias made his move. He said goodnight to Shirley and headed to bed in the private suite, up on the second floor. Only, first, he popped out to the shed that stored firewood. There were a few interesting tools in there, but one happened to be a small hand axe. He ran a finger along the blade and could see and feel that it had recently been sharpened. He returned to the staircase and made his way up, not to the 2$^{nd}$ floor living quarters, but to the first floor. Room 19.

He had a skeleton key for every single room. Suffering from a combination of jealous rage and drink, he opened the door and went inside. Tobias waited, standing in the middle of the room, questioning his sanity and why he was in there. Deep down he knew, but didn't want to admit it. He waited, listening to the corridor outside. Nothing but the occasional bit of laughter from downstairs. Then, the giggle, the sniggering and eager footsteps.

He walked calmly into the bathroom suite, pulling the door closed in the dark, waiting. The axe clenched tightly. The bedroom door key clattered in the lock and the door flew open. The giggles enraging him further. The couple started to manically undress, and he could hear kissing, shuffling and then the couple flew themselves onto the bed. The sounds coming through the bathroom door were exacerbating his anger, rage and conviction. The moment chosen, he threw the door open, and, in the gloom, he could see two naked bodies, writhing on the bed. The alcohol made them oblivious to his presence. He walked over to the bed, slowly, the sounds of drunk passion, enraging him further.

Tobias raised the axe and brought it down with all his might, contacting the back of the man's head, blood splattering into his face as the back of his victim's head opened up. The man fell silent.

Shirley, tried to raise a scream but her lovers body fell flat onto her, his head striking her cheek. Her sounds were stifled. Tobias grabbed the man's blood-soaked hair, moving his lifeless head aside.

The axe raised once more, and he struck it down into her face, clipping the man's ear as it went, blood pouring out. Again, another strike, then another, Shirley stopped moving, her beauty violently erased forever. She joined her casual fling in eternal sleep. The murderous act was done.

The most ridiculous thing afterwards was, Tobias dragged the two lifeless bodies from the bed. This was no easy task for a man of his age. He dragged them into the bathroom, one after the other. He took the time to change the bedding, using fresh bedclothes from the linen cupboard out in the hallway. He never intended to hide or cover up the brutal act. He never even intended on cleaning up the blood-spattered wallpaper. His intention was to try to erase the bond between the two victims, an irrational move by a madman. Tobias made his way through the dim lit corridor to his 2$^{nd}$ floor private quarters. He was aware that his clothing was blood soaked, but it was now late, and most of the soldiers and their guests were long gone. He got to his sanctuary, not knowing what to do next. The awful crime wasn't planned. There was no escape plan, and no real cover-up. He opened a new bottle of Whiskey and sat on the balcony. He drank slowly but steadily, one after the other. Another bottle was opened.

The next morning, the grim discovery was made. Tobias had fallen from the second-floor rear balcony onto the slate slabs below. Shortly after, the bodies were discovered in room 19. There was a note left wrapped and pushed into the second bottle of Whiskey, touching the half-filled contents that he couldn't drink. It Read:

*So, this is what it looks like. The last remainder of my life. I'm broken, jealous and very drunk. I did not want this to occur. I was loved and I loved too. The blasted voice won't go away. "DO IT! DO IT! DO IT! KILL THEM!" Am I mad, crazy, or possessed? I don't know, I don't care, it is done. I am done.... YES, I HEAR YOU Demon!!!*

# Chapter five

Bruce was feeling a little tiddly after his bottles of lager. His on-line search had been interesting.
He was starting to see a pattern of events that had occurred at the hotel. The place was starting to give up her secrets. The night was closing in and he decided to head up for an early night.

He climbed into bed, thoughts bouncing around his head. At one point it all just seemed too good to be true. He was certainly eager to get his hands on Dunella and the money. It looked like that was all going to happen, without any hiccups. He lay staring at the ceiling, the image of the shadow at the window was causing him to lay awake. For a long time, he decided to keep his bedside table lamp on.

Sunday morning arrived. The early morning sun, bathing his bedroom. He had not slept well. The image from the window and the internet search had left him very unsettled. He sat up and reached over to the little bedside table, pulling the single drawer open. His last packet of cigarettes stashed just in case. He was clearly stressing about the past few days' events. He prised the lid off the packet and pulled out a Super king. Benson and Hedges, his favourite. He pulled one out and ran it along his nose, back and forwards, breathing in the sweet smell of tobacco.

Tempted to get up and light it up, he placed it away, and put them back, slamming the drawer shut. Another time proven practice that he loved, was a steamy hot shower, first thing. Apart from a good run, nothing came close to it. Squaddies often find themselves, licking wounds in the shower, so to speak. Afterwards, he got ready, made his way downstairs, and clicked on the kettle. He was aware that tomorrow he had to go back to work. Unsure what to say. He thought about telling all, then as soon as he had that thought, he dismissed it. He opened his favourite messy drawer. Every kitchen has one. This one, underneath the cutlery drawer, was like a mini shed. It was filled with screw drivers, fuses and business cards, to name but a few items. In amongst the junk was his little notepad. It was time to list a few things and to form a plan.

He stared down at the bland paper; this was technically going to be the biggest thing he had to sort, for years. Life in the military had always been so black and white. Early morning wake-up calls, early morning run, barrack jobs. These were very tedious. Known as 'block jobs.' These were an integral part of a soldier's daily routine. Once the training for that day was completed, it was back to barracks to square away any untidiness around the place. Principally that meant wandering around the accommodation block, looking for any forms of litter. The inside jobs were usually about cleaning dorms and making sure the showers weren't hiding anything other than the odd bar of soap, or mislaid shampoo. These chores took up a lot of time and were and still are designed to instil discipline and a feeling of responsibility.

Ultimately all of this makes for a better type of person. That person primed and ready to take orders into battle. The problem with that is, once the daily ritual ends, so many can't cope out in the civilian world. This can lead veterans to turn to addiction. Many of his friends had done just that. At one point, he had been to more funerals related to suicide, than were related to deployment casualties. He was worried about all of this.

**The Notes:**
*1. Inform Major Jennings at HR of my decision to resign.*
*2. Serve three months' notice or go earlier?*
*3. Re-open Dunella or sell her as she is?*

*4. Take the money and the sale proceeds and start a new life!*
*5. Carry on at work for two more years.*

He went over them again and again. Number 4 was standing out the most. 'But where would I go?' he thought to himself. The first one would be difficult enough. This would signify the end to a decorated career of almost 30 years. He slammed the pen down and headed to the fridge. The beer was drunk. There was only one option lest as his hands started to shake again. He rummaged around the kitchen drawer, the one hiding his last cigarette. It was the only one way he had to calm down. He swung the back door open as he had done so many times before and lit it up. He drew on the cigarette and instantly calmed down. He had arrived at his decision.

Monday had arrived. Bruce dressed up in his military combat kit for work. He had overlooked his boots because of all the other stuff going on. They usually shone good enough to see spots on your face. Today they were taking second place. It had rained hard, and the 10-minute cycle awaited. Something he had been doing by habit for so long, felt like such a chore. He cycled a little slower than usual, his hands freezing up with chilly rain. He was about halfway there when he realised something else. He had forgotten his packed lunch. This was another trait of a long-time soldier, too many years of base food, is never recommended. The camp entrance appeared in the distance. He steered his bike into the side gate, just by the main gate to sign in.

"Morning sir," said the guard at the gate. Bruce pulled his MOD 90 out, for identification.

"Morning, still as handsome as ever I think!" he joked.

"Yeah, all good sir, your aware of the 1pm meeting today?" said the guard.

Bruce nodded, looking directly at the guard. He realised that he had completely forgotten about any meeting. The guard handed him his card back.

"Everything alright this morning sir?"

"Errr, yeah all's well, thank you 'oh...this meeting, same as usual, block B?" asked Bruce, searching for a bit of information to help jog his memory.

"No Sir, block B is closed for repairs. Block D, other side of the gym Sir!"

"Yes, how stupid of me, B is a disaster, good stuff, and have a good one,"

He locked his bike away in the bike shed just to the side of the main gate and started his daily short 2-minute walk along the path. Heading towards his office of duty as usual, he noticed a few more soldiers ambling around. More so than usual. There were troops sitting on a few unusually parked up armoured vehicles, namely The Jackal and Coyote vehicles. The army had been sending troops back to the United Kingdom from oversees, mainly Germany. Leuchars, home of The Royal Dragoon Guards, wasn't spared from the military draw- down. The garrison was usually home to several other units, not just the light cavalry. The REME and RMP regiments had units on camp. These combined with Bruce's' regiment's members meant there were some 1800 personnel on and local to camp. He passed another vehicle; there were two corporals and an officer in some sort of altercation. He carried on, ignoring them as best he could. But then:

"Oh, hello old boy, you based here, are you?" the posh, English educated voice said. The voice belonged to an officer.

Bruce stopped, and for a moment a voice inside his head reminded him that this was an officer addressing him. A tall man smartly turned out, boasting one pip, indicated he was a recent and most likely an inexperienced 2nd Lieutenant. Bruce offered a salute; it was reciprocated.

"Sir, I am indeed, how may I help you?"

"Look old boy, I don't mean to be a pain, but my men are on a temporary billet here, and I'm getting nowhere fast; all seems a little disorganised staff sergeant?"

The officer recognising his insignia as a staff sergeant, was searching for his sur-name.

"Sir, I am staff sergeant Gordon, what seems to be up?"

"I am Lieutenant Moxley, are we supposed to sit here on the roadside or are we going to be shown where to park up?"

Bruce looked along the line of armoured vehicles, six or seven in all and troops kicking about restlessly.

"Where have you arrived from Sir?"

"We are part of the draw down from Osnabruck Garrison, there's more of us on-route," he said. For a moment or two, Bruce felt like walking on and sending the young officer on a snail trail to find out what was going on for himself. However, it all came flooding back to him. The meeting due at 1pm that day, was to address the short notice return of 300 troops, 15 lorries and 26 armoured vehicles. He was back in the game for now and had to put Dunella away for a while. "Leave it with me sir, I'll speak to the guardroom now and get you all moved on base asap."

Bruce did exactly that, he went back to the gatehouse to see what had been going on. It seemed that the sergeants tasked with the accommodation block housing had run into a few issues. The camp had been under-going a modernisation uplift. It swelled in size over the past few years, mainly due to the regiment's involvement in Afghanistan and the European withdrawal. The new blocks, put up especially for such numbers had been delayed. They were built and very well, but the gas boilers had not yet been tested and given the green light. There were other issues with laundry areas or lack of. Other problems were related to electrical safety commissioning. All of this was what the 1pm meeting was intending to address.

Bruce reassured the officer that all was in hand. One of the missing sergeants would be back soon enough with instructions for his men. He carried on up to his office block and arrived a little late, due to the involvement with the new arrivals. The usual receptionist was at her desk typing frantically. "Morning Chloe, all good?" he asked.

Chloe didn't take her eyes off the screen.

"Hey there's a familiar voice; morning to you too Sir," she replied.

Bruce noted the time on the back of the dusty bronze wall clock behind reception. It was now 9.25am He was late! Late is something he never ever participated in. 'A first' he thought for everything.

"So, how's the belly?" asked Chloe.

"The belly, what's up with it?" replied Bruce.

"You tell me, you called in sick Friday, remember?"

He had all but forgotten. The weekend had washed so many normal thoughts away.

"Oh yes, was awful, I'm ok now though, much better thanks."

He headed down the corridor to his usual office, secretly hoping that Captain Welham was off. He knew that the time was coming to have the conversation. Captain Welham, or Mikey as he preferred to be called, was a stout man. He had worked his way up through the ranks similarly to Bruce. Known for his drinking sessions more than anything else, he was however a very experienced soldier and officer. Mikey had several tours under his belt. Iraq, Afghanistan, Kosovo, Cyprus, Sudan, to name but a few. Just like Bruce, his superiors had done a super job of sending them to serve in the world's greatest shite holes.

He got to the door and stopped for a moment. He couldn't hear a sound and just waited to compose himself. 'Do I say something today? Or wait?' he thought. He wanted to get it over with but was nervous about any decision. He opened the door and looked around to his right, the coast was clear. He scampered over to his desk, set on the left of the room, for a moment feeling relief that he was alone. It was approaching 10am. The big meeting was due for 1pm. There were things to sort out, paperwork to check and online docs to prepare. This was a typical day for Bruce. The bullets and bombs swapped for ink, paper and his PC.

He sat down and leaned on his elbows for a time. He was trying to get back in the game, thinking about the young Lieutenant and his men, soon to arrive on base. He glanced over to the corner mini kitchenette area and knew it was going to be a 'plenty of caffeine' type of day.

Suddenly the office door swung open, it was Mikey.

"Ahh, Bruce, how are you feeling now?" he asked. He sat down at his desk, focusing on his PC.

"All good, I'm much better thanks." He took a couple of mugs out of the cupboard and put two heaped spoons of coffee into both. His colleague liked strong coffee just as much, only he had his black with four sugars. Bruce was a more 'plenty of milk' type of guy. He passed the coffee to Mikey and sat back at his desk, his head a wash with thoughts. He started to scroll down on his PC, looking for relevant notes he may have made regarding the meeting due. Mikey was slurping on his coffee, irritating at the best of times. "Had you eaten something a bit dodge Bruce?"

He peered over his monitor. "Um, possibly, you know what the food can be like on camp," he said.

"Aye, I do, I can say there were a few lads taken ill a couple of weeks ago, bloody kitchens." said Mikey.

Bruce knew he had to keep to his story and was more than happy to do so.

"I think I have got a wee bit sensitive as I've got older." He changed the subject.

"Mikey, are you up to speed with the meeting later?"

"Aye, all good here, and you?"

"Erm, not really, can we work together on this, I wasn't myself over the weekend," He paused, and hoped for a helpful response.

"It's no issue pal; you just attend, and I'll do most of the talking. We need to get the newly arrived squared away; into the new blocks."

"Great, you're right, we need to help these guys, blasted contractors!" he said. Bruce thought about telling him his news. He kept on dismissing it, but he knew now was as good as ever. He finished off the last of his coffee. "Mikey, I have a bit of news to share with you," he said, his left hand starting to shake again. He could here Mikey shifting his chair to swing by the monitor.

"Oh, what's that? You won the lottery pal?"

"Not quite, but I'll be honest, I might as well have done." he replied.

Mikey now intrigued, rolled his office chair around the table and focused on Bruce.

"You what? What's gone on?"

The cat was out of the bag. He wanted to brag about his good fortune. He also didn't want to share it at all. What he did know, was that it had to come out soon. The time was now.

"My auntie, she passed away recently. I've come into a bit of good fortune," he said, wiping a bead of sweat from his forehead.

"Tell me, what have you done? You got an inheritance or something?"

"I do indeed, substantial, it's enough for me to think about my position here Mikey." His hand calmed a bit, and he got up to head to the kettle again. Mikey was still sat by the end of his desk, fiddling with his boot laces. "You want another one?" referring to another coffee.

"I think I need one after your revelation-you really thinking of chucking your beret in?" He wheeled back to his usual place.

Bruce nervously poured the kettle and prepared the coffees; he handed one to Mikey, spilling a bit on his desk.

"Oops, sorry mate, my bad, I'll get a cloth," he said nervously.

"Don't worry, its fine, there we go, no worries," said Mikey, he wiped the coffee spill with the forearm of his shirt. He let out a short whistle, impatient with Bruce's' slow approach to the news. Bruce sat down again.

"Times against us pal, spit it out!" said Mikey.

"Ok, I now own a hotel and its wonderful, oh and a sum of money, that's it." It was out. The news was passed on. The room fell silent for a few moments. "Bloody hell Bruce, are you kidding me on?"

"I'm not, it's true, I'm trying to come to terms with this." he replied.

"Come to terms with it?

Well, you should be celebrating, not so down in the dumps!"

Bruce took a moment or two to gather himself and for a moment he wondered why he wasn't so excited about it.

"I am over the moon, I really am. The thing is, it comes with a price to pay," he said.

"And what's the price to pay?" Mikey was keen to know more and already a little envy had sunk in.

"The end of my career, that's what, I wasn't intending on going just yet."

It was almost 12pm by now. They had talked a great deal about his revelation. Mikey was very interested and also, he expressed a sadness that his colleague may be about to announce his resignation. They had drunk copious amounts of caffeine, a standard practice for the office personnel. They had also realised that little had been achieved with preparation for the 1pm meeting. They focused back on the job in hand, printing off a few A4 sheets of guidelines and directions for the troop commanders.

The meeting was upon them. The usual questions were asked, and the usual answers were given. The situation was sorted, with all the available accommodation blocks cleared for safe habitation. Bruce had engaged well enough, but his head wasn't in it at all. Mikey could sense this but wasn't surprised. After the meeting, they headed back to the office.

"Great, that's another fine job done Bruce," said Mikey.

He was at the kettle again, suffering a slight headache from lack of caffeine, even if it was only an hour and a bit since his last one.

He poured two mugs and offered one to Mikey.

"Yep, another fine example of sorting out a typical military cock up," he replied.

"Indeed, and the sort of thing you have been great at doing Bruce."

He thought about that statement for a few moments. He was good at this job, but he had been much better at being a soldier in the field. A soldier on active duty, engaged in combat operations. He was never cut out for the office. Unfortunately, this is the fate for most long- career soldiers. If they haven't promoted to such a rank by a certain age, they are usually discharged. The army had a certain way of ushering such soldiers out of a job. It was known that the mundane life behind the desk, would affect them to the point of resignation.

After all, a soldier who has spent his career doing what soldiers are trained for, suddenly faces a desk and a computer, would sift out the ones that could adapt well. The ones that couldn't, usually about fifty percent would resign. The army calculated a huge saving in salary terms when they drop like flies.

"So, what are you going to do?" asked Mikey.

Without hesitation, Bruce responded with his heartfelt reply.

"I'm going to put in my notice and hang up my boots."

The decision came with little hesitation. He knew that the opportunity awaiting him was just too good to let it sit on the fence. To get the hotel ready for business and give her the attention she demanded. He had to go.

# Chapter six

He hoped the following three months would pass by relatively quickly, but he knew that it would more than likely drag on. He waited a full week before handing his official notice in. The morning arrived soon enough where he went to see major Jennings; formal letter in hand. As expected, major Jennings tried all he could to get Bruce to think again, but his mind was made up. The offer was given to him to take the 3$^{rd}$ month off due to accrued holiday, so he only had to work two of the three months' notice period. He was more than satisfied with that, knowing that the sooner he got to grips at Dunella the better.

Just a few weeks after Bruce formally resigned, he had word from the solicitor and the estate agent. Everything went through very quickly. The legal work was done, the grant of probate in the will was finalised. He was now the legal owner of Dunella and better off by the tune of £125,000, minus costs, taxes etc.

There was only one more month to serve. He had received the good news that the keys were with the estate agent. The day had arrived where he met with the agent one more time. It was a wet and dreary Monday afternoon. He left the base a bit earlier than usual and headed straight for the agents. This time he was going to pick up the keys. He got to the entrance door and peered through. He could see Cindy. She was on the telephone, but she noticed Bruce, frantically waving her hand ushering him in. He entered and stood a few feet from her desk.

"Hi Mr Gordon, be with you in a sec, take a seat," she said, still chatting on the phone. He sat in a comfy chair at the side of the room. He thought how similar it all looked, like a dentist's waiting room. There was a small circular table in the middle of a few chairs.

On this was a pile of magazines. Bruce had a flick through the one at the top. 'Home and gardens.' He flicked through, looking at the beautiful pictures of grand buildings, surrounded by gorgeous gardens. This sort of thing never used to interest him. He was more interested in 'What Car' or 'Soldier' magazines. He peeped over the top of the magazine, wishing that Cindy would end the call. He couldn't help but notice how gorgeous she was looking today. Her long dark brown hair, encompassing her pale flawless skin. All encompassed in a tight red with black pin striped business suit.

Eventually his 'carried away' state was shattered.

"Hey Mr Gordon, good to see you," she called over. "Grab a seat, we have a few things to go through." He placed the magazine back and tidied the pile. With a spring in his step, he took up the offer and sat opposite Cindy. "Ok, how have you been?" she asks.

"Really well, been looking forward to this for a while, happy its almost done," he replied, nervously clasping his slightly sweaty palms.

"Good to hear and it's all done, she's all yours from 3pm today."

Cindy pulled an A4 brown envelope from the desk drawer. She tore it open, revealing copies that were made at the solicitor's office. She placed them down, going through several copies meticulously. There was an awkward silence as she studied them, the only sound in the office, another male colleague arguing on the phone with someone. Bruce noted the time, 11.35am. Soon, in just a few hours, his life would change.

"Right, this one sign here, and here, this one sign here and here and while you're doing that, I'll grab the keys," she said. He read through some of the jargon, choosing to miss out most of it. The excitement was hitting home. The paperwork was just his authority tied with the solicitors, enabling the agent to release the keys. He placed the paperwork back on Cindy's side and sat back to relax. He could hear the jangle and chink of keys.

"That's your bunch, sure they are all here," she said, laying a large bunch on the desk. There were several keys, your typical selection of Yale and traditional mortice keys. He hesitated, waiting for permission.

"That's it Mr Gordon, the keys are yours."

"Wow, a handsome set they are too," he said.

"Yes, the entrance lobby, and a couple of out-buildings. I believe Archie has put the room and office keys in the safe in the back office."

She finished off with opening a small white envelope. This one revealed the alarm instructions and the combination to the safe. The formalities over, they shook hands, wishing him luck. He headed home.

Home for now, was the military two bed house he had been used to for many years. As part of the arrangement with the army, he had a full six months to maintain rent on the property. The initial three months as part of the notice period would soon be over. He could give up the property at any time. If all went well, he would soon be living on the second floor, in the private suite at Dunella. This was one of the rooms yet to be explored.

There was still the question of the apartment he owned in Broughty. This was purchased years ago and rented out. The mortgage was quite high, and the rent was quite low, comparably. The idea was always to have the place as an investment put towards his retirement. There was little point in keeping the apartment now. He had plans to sell it. For now, that really was the least of his worries. After all, the inheritance now realised put any worries about that behind him....at least for now.

He pulled into his drive, as usual. He noticed the bottom corner of the nosey neighbour's curtain gently falling back. This was a common theme when he left or returned. Until now, he had bottled it all up about his good fortune. He was determined to keep it that way, for as long as possible. Somehow, he knew that Jimmey would figure it out, he always did. He went inside and headed straight to the kettle. Placing the paperwork and the bunch of keys on the kitchen table, he let out a long sigh. A sigh of relief and excitement.

After all, it's not every day you become the owner of a hotel and life changing amounts of cash. Pouring an extra strong coffee, he sat down and stared at the keys. He was experiencing a feeling of euphoria and of anxiety all in one. The realisation hitting home about leaving the army. He drank the coffee, going over the paperwork. Taking a notepad out from the messy drawer, he noted the alarm code and the safe combination.

His mobile started to ring, a Nokia 6210, not a bad choice at that time. Bruce did not recognise the number, letting it ring a little longer than he usually would.

"Hello, Bruce here."

"Mr Gordon, it...its Archie, I hear you're the proud new owner of Dunella!" he said.

"Hey, Archie, I am indeed, got there in the end; you been, ok?"

The phone went quiet for a moment: "I am good Mr Gordon; I was just wondering when your doon at the hotel next?" he asked, his strong Scots accent proving a bit of a barrier for Bruce. He was intending on going to the hotel that evening. "Well, I was thinking of going up there in a couple of hours' time."

"Ah, ok, that's great Mr Gordon, what sort of time exactly?"

Bruce noted it was now 3,30pm, the sooner the better to go there he thought. He was like a little child with a new toy, impatient to say the least. "I'm heading there at five-ish; should be there before half past."

"Great I'll see you then if that's ok Mr Gordon?" said Archie.

"Totally fine by me...er is everything ok?"

"Ok.... um yeah, all good, I just want to get you sorted, you know, with the keys and things. Will that be ok with you?" Bruce paused for a few moments, realising that in actual fact, it would be nice to have someone else there, especially if it starts to get dark.

"No problem at all, and its Bruce to you, not Mr, ok Archie?" he said.

"Righteo Mr....um Bruce, that's great, I'll see you aroond 5.30."

"Yep, see you there, take care till then." The stage was set, the long-awaited return to Dunella was a reality. Bruce couldn't contain his inner child. He was becoming more excited by the minute. In just a couple of hours' time, he would be back at the grand hotel, this time as the rightful new keeper. He scurried around the house, searching for his little tool kit. He thought that from now on he would need to go prepared. The old building and all her doors and windows, locks and countless other such things, would no doubt require adjustment. He located his bag, stuffed in the under-stair's cupboard. He thought it best to throw in a can of wd40, retrieved from the messy kitchen drawer.

Suddenly the doorbell goes. He had just been in the hallway under the stairs. Right now, he wasn't in the mood for visitors and only cared about the early evening meet at Dunella. He hesitated for a time, peering around the kitchen door to the hall. He could see the shadow of someone. He waits, wishing them to go. But it rings again, a longer burst this time.

He had little choice; his car was on the drive.

"BE RIGHT THERE!" he shouts out. He closed up the kit bag, placing it on the kitchen table. He approached the door through the hall, the bell sounding again.

"Yes, yes God's sake," he said under his breath, opening the front door.

Stood, semi sheltering from a now rainy late afternoon, was Mr nosey bag of the century.

"Oh, hi Bruce, sorry to bother you, have you got a couple of minutes?" 'Typical' thought Bruce. "Yes, a couple, I'm busy at the moment, what's up Jimmey?" he asks. He leans towards the door, glancing up at the rain, not too heavy rain.

"Bloody weather, um, can I come in for a minute?" he asks.

Bruce didn't want to appear harsh and considering the now intensifying downpour, he obliged. They stood for a moment too long in the hallway.

"Come through Jimmey, what can I do for you?"

"Everything ok with you lately Bruce?" he asks in his usual curious tone of voice; following Bruce through to the kitchen.

"What do you mean?" replies Bruce.

"Oh, you tend to tell when somethings up around here, you know?"

"Like what exactly?"

"Well, you are showing signs of irregularity!"

Bruce made a decision to be nice, not to snap, not to usher him out. He thought that actually, Jimmey was right. He had been going to and from all manner of office and not to mention Dunella.

Bruce joined Jimmey at the kitchen table, who was already sat down.

"It's just, you are not sticking to your usual military style of routine, and I've known you for some years now. I just wanted to make sure that all's well." Bruce got up and darted over to his favourite watering hole. The kettle switched on: "Tea, coffee?"

"I'd love cup of tea, if you have time?" The kettle boiled, the tea was poured and another coffee at the ready. 'What do I tell him?' thought Bruce. To his surprise, for the moment, it seemed his neighbour was genuinely concerned. He knew that he had to know sooner or later.

"I just thought you may be ill, or you know, something?"

"Me?" he replied. "I'm strong as an Ox me!"

"Maybe a woman has come into Bruce's life?" Jimmey asked. He handed Jimmey the tea and sat back down. His overly curious neighbour had a knack for sussing things out. The same dilemma hit home just before he told all the Mikey prior to announcing his resignation.

Bruce leaned back into the chair and took a long slurp on his still very hot coffee. A voice entering his head saying, 'keep quiet' another 'tell him.' This was Bruce, rationalising the whole thing.

"I do have some news Jimmey, all good, nothing at all to worry about. I put my notice in a few weeks ago, I'm leaving the army."

Jimmey was taking down his own gulp of tea and choked slightly at the news.

"What? You're not serious?"

"I am, it is done-I'll be out in a few weeks, and soon after I'll be moving," he said. Jimmey's eyes were almost popping out of their sockets; this was perfect gossip for him to stew over.

"But your career, your home, what's led you to this?"

"I have come into a bit of luck, and don't worry, I'll not be too far away." It was out of the bag; it seemed that taking on Dunella was never going to be a secret. Bruce took another sip and looked across at Jimmey. He could see him computing the information. His nosey nature, causing his head to boil. Bruce waited for the next salvo of questions.

"Ah, ok, local you say, where to?"

"The ferry, not far," he replies.

"As in Broughty?"

Bruce let out a quick breath, preparing for the next question.

"New job?"

"Sort of, yes, like I said not too far. I'll tell you, but you need to promise me that it won't become common knowledge around here?" Jimmey tilted his head slightly and grinned, sipping at his tea, locking eyes with Bruce.

"What will you be doing Mr military man?" he asked, on the lookout for more info. Bruce hadn't even started.

"I'll be running a hotel." Jimmey almost chokes on his tea and continues with: "You are shitting me, right?"

"No, I'm not shitting you, I am the proud new owner of Dunella hotel."

Jimmey falls unusually silent; the reply from Bruce stumps his questioning tactics for a few moments. But soon enough...

"Bloody hells bells, are you serious?"

Bruce grins back at him, almost enjoying his shock horror at the information. "Yes, I am not making this up, why would I? If you don't mind, I have to meet someone there soon Jimmey."

"But how has this happened, have you bought it?" asks Jimmey.

"No, not on my salary, that place is worth a bomb. I have inherited her and that's that." An hour or so had passed, he had one more to go before meeting Archie at Dunella. He made polite excuses for gently kicking him out. As he walked the hallway, a further salvo of curiosities were asked. Bruce gently declined further, saying he had an important meeting, finishing off with: 'Now you know why my movements have been different.' With Jimmey now gone, he came to terms that 3pm had passed. He was officially and legally the owner, and from today, his life would be taking a brand-new direction. His heart started to pound again, the anxiety that coincided with the massive realisation causing him to fluctuate between happiness and a feeling of doubt. This journey was going to be crazy. It was going to be exciting. Little did he know at this point; it was also going to be a living nightmare.

It was almost 5pm, he grabbed the bunch of keys and the envelope with the all-important alarm code and safe combination. While locking the front door, he did the usual peer around the front, just to see if Jimmey was about. This time, the coast was clear. He set off, with a feeling of excitement, usually owned by children on a birthday or Christmas day. After all, it's not everyone who suddenly has a huge hotel and s decent amount of cash, from nowhere. The drive to the Broughty Ferry was a nice 15 minutes on a good day, 20 at a push. He noticed that his hands on the steering wheel were unusually clammy, a sure sign of anxiety.

On the way, many thoughts were passing through his head. Thoughts from his childhood stay at Dunella. Thoughts about the army and all the great times. Thoughts about the mountain ahead of him, attempting to resurrect an old business. He was thinking about hiring staff, but before that, there was sprucing up to do, painting here and there, and furnishings. Although it was a good thing that Archie had been doing most of that before and after the closure. One thought bothered him the most. That was the image of a certain shadowy figure that appeared at that window. This wouldn't go away and had been on his mind a great deal. The conversation he had with Aunt Alices' friend who picked up the settee. The subject being all about a spiritualist church and similar creepy things. He tried to put all of these out of mind, for the time-being. He was almost there, turning onto Albany Road.

    He pulled into the large opening of the driveway. This time it seemed very different as he drove around the deserted circular drive. He parked just to the left of the reception area and switched off the engine. It was a bright early evening, warm and birds singing. He got out of the car and leaned against it, taking the view in. There she was in all her glory. It was almost 5.30pm, the plan to get there for that time went perfectly. There was no sign of Archie just yet. He wandered towards the entrance but decided to take a turn left. This led to the back carpark area. He thought it would be a good thing to have a mooch around, especially because there wasn't time with Cindy the first time around.

    He walked through the main carpark along a cobbled pathway. On his left was a tennis court. He stopped to muse through the chain-link fencing. The court was green and looked in decent condition. The only thing was, that the new was not there and there were the odd pile of brown leaves, swirling about in a breeze. Beyond the court he could see an archway, some ten feet tall, covered in a mix of Rose and Ivy bush. The carpark on his right was devoid of vehicles, only a bicycle rack was harbouring an abandoned bike.

    He got to the arch and proceeded through. On the other side, he could see a small pond and just over to the right of that one, was another. He walked around the first pond, looking in at the murky water. The water was still and seemed devoid of life. There were a couple of Lilypad's, and surface weed. He noticed how quiet the whole place was, and a bit eerie. The ponds were semi hidden with overhanging shrubs and untidy bushes to the rear of the grounds. He looked back at the hotel. For the first time he could see her, stood handsomely in the diminishing evening light. Between the ponds and the back of the building, laid a sprawling green lawn. He estimated it was about 60 metres away having a good judge of distance from his army target range days. Dunella looked incredible. The front with the driveway was great but the rear seemed to be a hidden gem. There were two circular towers, one either side of her. These gave the feeling that Dunella was straight out of a fairy-tale story. Bruce stood there, taking in the view, soaking up the birdsong and contemplating about so much.

    He decided to go back to the entrance, hoping Archie would by now be there. As he stepped off, he stepped on something, causing the object to snap. He lifted his foot up, crouching down to pick it up. It was a small wooden frame, about six inches square. Upon this was a dirty brass plaque.

    He rubbed the dirt off o his trousers, and could just about make out the scroll writing:

*In loving memory of a fine gardener who poured her heart and soul into Dunella. Maureen is much missed but is here in spirit forever more*

A chill ran up and down his spine. He recalled Cindy mentioning an incident with a gardener, but at this point he didn't know too much more. He sensed that Cindy was not telling him the whole truth. He headed back along a path, one of two that ran either side of the lawn. He carried the plaque with him, hoping that soon as he could get hold of some Brasso, he would give it a clean-up and polish. He walked over the patio area, made from a mid-grey slate-coloured slabs and around to the entrance. There was still no sign of Archie. It was now 6pm. He thought to wait a few more minutes then give him a call. However, in the excitement to get there he had left his mobile on the kitchen table. He stepped up onto the entrance terrace and peered through one of the double doors. He closed his hands around his face to get a better look.

'That looks bloody creepy,' he thought, praying that Archie would turn up. Suddenly a shrill screech, coming from the rear gardens. He had just come from there and the noise was loud enough to make him freeze to the spot. He leaned around from the door, not daring to move. Then:

"Hey Mr Gordon, apologies I'm late," the voice said. Startled, he turned to see Archie, just a few feet away, having turned up almost silently on a bicycle. He propped the bike up against a marble looking column.

"Flaming hell Archie, you scared the living daylights out of me," said Bruce. They shook hands.

"What was that awful shrill scream out the back?"

"That was probably Freya, nothing to worry about, she's tame-ish."

"Who the hell's Freya?"

Archie paused for a moment, reaching into his small rucksack.

"That would be one of our fox family. They are around here, don't worry Mr Gordon," he said, removing a cycle clip from his right ankle. Another shrill scream sound came, making Bruce look over his shoulder. He had heard some strange animal sounds before, but the fox scream, is something else. "So, she's all yours now Mr Bruce?" said Archie, fiddling with something in his rucksack. He pulled out a torch, switching it on and off a couple of times, making sure it was working.

"A couple things Archie, first, call me Bruce, second, why the torch?"

"Well, Bruce, the torch; Dunella has a mind of her own at times, you never know when she'll shut doon the power. Archie closed his bag and peered through the double doors.

"It's quiet in there the noo," he said.

"Quiet, its closed!" replied Bruce.

"Aye, she's closed, but she's not always at peace." Archie pulled out a set of keys and rattled the main one in the lock. Bruce didn't elaborate on the 'peace' comment, thinking it was just an 'Archie' type of remark. The door opened, creaking on the old hinges, and the usual loud alarm reset bleep engaged. Archie rushed over to the alarm panel and punched in the appropriate numbers. The alarm was silenced.

"I'm pleased you did that Archie; I would have flapped with the buttons."

"Oh, you'll soon get it Bruce, it's easy after a few tries." Archie pushed through the sprung hinged inner double doors. Leading into the main reception. Inside the main hall, the air seamed stale, since the first time with Cindy. There was a damp smell in the air, nipping his nostrils. He realised that she was obviously wearing a strong perfume that day, improving the stale air more than he'd realised. Archie went to the back of the reception desk and placed his bag on the counter. Bruce took a few moments to look around. This time it seemed different. This time, he was the owner, and underlying was an anxiety that he couldn't explain. Perhaps it was the subconscious realisation that the responsibility was all his. He peered up the grand staircase, noting that it looked gloomier in the early evening light. And as if by magic, the lighting came on. Archie called him through into the back office.

"There we are, the safe is open, and it requires a lot of sorting out," he said. Bruce stood in the office as Archie pulled small brown envelopes out.

"These are the room keys, and these are for you." He handed over another set of keys. A small gold key fob with two initials on it... 'PS.'

"What's PS?"

"That's you're living accommodation, 'Private Suite'; hopefully it was left clean and tidy."

Bruce watched him as he methodically moved around the office, switching on switches and clinking sets of keys. There was another large key safe on the back wall, just by an old-fashioned looking desk. He opened the safe revealing what looked like hundreds of keys, all sizes but seemingly in order, with a tag on each one. He moved his index finger along each line, finally arriving at a particular key with a red tag on it.

"There we are," he said breathing a sigh of relief. "This is for your eyes-only Bruce." He hands Bruce a worn looking old-fashioned key, a dull grey colour.

"Oh, what's this for?" asks Bruce.

"Now, that one is for the new owner. In the PS room, there's a safe, hidden behind the bed board." He placed the key in his jean pocket, wondering about the safe upstairs. With the key-safe closed again, Archie headed off towards the main lobby, quietly muttering something illegible. Bruce followed, admiring the slick actions Archie employed, showing how familiar with Dunella he really was. Bruce leaned against the reception desk while Archie vanished into a cupboard just to the underside of the grand staircase. Moments later he reappeared with news:

"Great, the water is turned on, the electric was already on, all the trip switches are on inside the distribution board and all seems well."

"Great stuff, Archie, I'd be lost without you."

"Aye, don't worry, we will go through a proper handover when things settle down here. There's a great deal to come to learn and it's a mix between old and new I'm afraid. Next in line, the Culloden Room. As before, Archie rattles a long key into the lock, entering the room. Bruce recalled that it was undergoing some redecoration works, and hoped it was complete. Upon entering, he could see all the dust sheets that were strewn around were gone. The paint tins that were here and there were removed and the air was filled with a fresh paint odour. Archie walked to the far end, just to the right-hand side of the stage. He pulled on a purple-coloured curtain, revealing a concealed door. Bruce followed, intrigued at yet another door.

"This is the cellar entrance," announced Archie.

"Wow, a cellar, great stuff, hope the lights are working down there."

"Should be good, the torch is on reception if we need it, don't worry, I got rid of the worse spiders!"

Archie pulled the door open; this one was a bit narrow and painted black. The sudden rush of stale air blew past them. It stank of stale beer and rotten eggs. Archie reached into the stairwell and the light turned on. That revealed a set of stone steps leading downward into the gunnels of Dunella. Bruce hadn't prepared for the smell, causing him to sneeze a few times as Archie ventured downwards.

"Oh dear, these ruddy steps are always so steep, hold onto the handrail Bruce."

"Will do, I'm not intending on busting an ankle just yet." They reached the bottom. Bruce realised that he could stand up properly. Cellars are normally quite claustrophobic with low ceilings. This one was very different and quite a surprise. It was reasonably well lit up too. There were beer lines fixed to the ceiling, heading up to the long bar in Culloden room. Typical of Archie, he had disappeared whilst Bruce was checking out the area. He could hear rattling and a scraping ahead. He walked forwards, noticing a few doors heading off left and right, along a corridor. The walls were bare stone and made from large blocks of contemporary grey granite. There were small square panes of glass in each door. He couldn't see anything beyond them, just darkness. Towards the end of the corridor, the scraping sound got louder, as he got closer to the end. The end of the corridor had three doors. One directly ahead and one either side. The doors were closed and like the others a dark stained wood. The curious little windows revealing dark rooms. For a few moments, the scraping noise stopped and from behind he could hear steps. It was Archie. "Sorry aboot that, I was having trouble getting the gas mains on," he said in his broad Scots accent. He opened one of the doors in the middle of the corridor, "Here I'll show you, this is all stuff you need to know aboot."

Archie walked into the room; Bruce followed closely. The room was lit up and he could see that there were curious little black curtains over the glass panes. In the corner was a bright yellow metal box, the door was open. Inside was a large handle with GAS clearly labelled on it.

"Right Bruce, this is one of the things that needs to be done from time to time. The gas was off, and the blasted handle was stiff as anything."

"Yeah, I heard the screeching, was eerie, but it was nothing but a stiff handle.

"Aye, bloody stiff and needs a good lube up, pardon the pun."

"Why is it down here?" asked Bruce, Archie closed the door.

"Well, that's a question for the previous owners. The original gas pipes were on this level and the mains have been here for years." Bruce was curious about the other doors, especially as they had the little curtains on them. He wanted to know why and what they were hiding.

"Why are these little curtains on the doors?"

"Those are to keep prying eyes out, that's all," replied Archie.

"Prying, what do you mean?"

"From trades and the like who may be doon here.

There's often new furniture, certain food boxes and electrical appliances in these rooms," he explained. They left the room. Archie locked the door behind him and turned towards the door at the end of the corridor, the one with adjacent doors either side. Typically, Archie rattled another key into the lock. Bruce looked around and back along to the bottom of the steps. He felt a bit uneasy and couldn't explain why. That part of the corridor was about ten metres long. The door swung open. As before, Archie entered, reaching inside for a switch. The light came on, albeit flickering this time. They entered the corridor. This time, Bruce could see ahead but the corridor turned to the right. The ceilings high enough like the others and dark stained wooden doorways on either side. Archie walked ahead and followed the corridor around. Bruce noticed a plunge in temperature, compared to the entrance way. Archie stopped and faced Bruce.

"Right, this is probably going to come as a surprise, but this whole part of the cellar was part of a holding cell block."

"A holding cell block, do you mean a prison?" asked Bruce.

"No, not a prison, more a temporary cell to house the unruly, long before Dunella became what she is the now. Early Broughty was a very busy port, bringing in all types from around the world." Bruce could see that the doors were the same as before, just timber, not bars or steel in any way.

"But the doors are not reinforced?"

"Aye, I know, but they were in the past and they were home to drunk sailors and stowaways and all manner of scum," he explained.

"So, none of this was mentioned in the meetings or the formal documentation, why?" Archie looked down at the cobbled floor, scraping a foot across from left to right.

"There are other secrets here Bruce, but it's too much for day one. The past is sometimes best left alone."

"So, the hotel is built on an old police station or what?"

"Not quite, an early establishment run by the local sheriff as they were once known. They were the earliest kind of police, before the police, if that makes sense."

"I don't believe this, it's cool right Archie?"

"Yes and no, cool,,,,maybe." He turned and walked a bit further, following the cold corridor around. Now that it was revealed as an old prison of sorts, Bruce could see that it was designed for such a purpose. The wooden doors would have been barred at one point. The rooms beyond each door were likely small cells, now used for storage or not.

"So, these rooms behind the doors, are they the old cells?"

"Aye, small, but the perfect size for a cell. These were early prototypes that more recent cells were based upon." Archie stopped at a random door and rattled a key into the lock. The door swung open revealing the cell. Bruce stared through the doorway at the room beyond. It was lit with a small single light bulb. There were boxes on the floor, labelled with trousers large, sweatshirt medium and skirts etc etc. The room was only three metres deep. There was little else to see apart from the remains of a metal bedframe, propped up on its side, springs hanging out in all directions.

"So, this one had staff clothing I see, which one has the bodies?" he asked Archie. He went quiet and Bruce could see his face turn very still and expressionless.

"Why would you say that?"

"I was only joking; I meant nothing by it."

"Dunella has many secrets Bruce, you'll learn to choose your words wisely." Bruce didn't quite know how to respond to that, so he didn't bother. The tour of the cellar came to an end, and the walk around the circular corridor ended with them going back into the entrance area. The warmer air was a relief, compared to the chill from further inside. They climbed back up the stone steps into the Culloden room. Archie locked the door and pulled the curtain back across the doorway, concealing the entrance once again.

Back inside the Culloden room, Bruce watched as Archie went behind the long bar, fiddling around as usual. Bruce upended a stacked barstool and sat at the bar. He noted that the bar had been cleaned well, since the viewing with Cindy. The back-bar was a bit bare. There were several optics dotted around and holders for spirits. He could see a fridge and a dishwasher, the typical bar type, a brown colour with silver edging. The mirrored back wall was clean and lit from small spotlights hidden within a recess. The bar as a whole, looked ready to go and the room appeared finished. He watched as Archie fiddled around with the newish looking till. He clicked on a couple of switches on the back wall, and it sprang into life. Archie concentrated on the till, opening and closing it a few times, listening for the bell ding each time.

"So, Archie, the bar, is it a money spinner?" asked Bruce.

"That's an understatement if ever I've heard one Bruce. On a good night the bar takes anything from £800 to £2000 pounds, give or take."

"OMG, that's a good amount, is there much profit on that?"

"Aye, plenty, if it's a wedding night or even just a wake, she always produces, good to see the till is fine," said Archie. He shuffled under the bar, producing a couple of boxes, a green one and a brown one, they were heavy as he rattled them. "I can't believe these are still here; I've been so embroiled with the painting I'd not noticed them." He lifts off the green lid from the tin. Inside are three rolls. They are money, 5s 10s and 20s.

"Wow, bingo!" said Bruce. Archie pulled the brown lid off, revealing numerous money bags. He pulled these out and were full of coins, some copper, the rest a mix of 50s 20s and 10s.

"Mr Gordon, this is the bar float, should have been put in the safe."

"How much is there?" asks Bruce.

"Usually two or three hundred, that's standard. It's all yours now."

"No, it's the bars, not mine, it will soon be used again hopefully Archie."

He put the contents back into the tins, sealing them tight. He made his way out of Culloden and across the reception lobby to the rear office. Bruce followed. Back in the office, Archie fiddled with the safe again, opening it up and placed the two boxes inside. "There, that's a better place for you two," he said. Archie sat at the office chair, to the back of the desk. a nice comfortable black leather one He turned around, looking out at the circular driveway. Bruce stood a bit awkwardly feeling that he was being undermined. He didn't know why he felt that way. It was probably because he knew that Archie was like the fixtures and fittings in the hotel. He held all the cards, all the secrets. Bruce knew that Archie may know other things, secrets, stories too and would decide to tell all when he saw fit. This made Bruce feel a bit like he was being kept in the dark. He had to trust Archie. He was the key to getting Dunella back up to speed and to get her trading as before. After all, a hotel that you own outright, must be a great money spinner, or so he thought.

Bruce had absolutely zero business experience. His army career was not at all to do with business, finance or managing a hotel. He had no knowledge of accounting staffing or indeed hiring and firing. Where do you start with no experience? These thoughts started to enter his head, and it made him feel 'out of his depth.' He knew that he would have to learn from Archie, take advice from him and listen in. Bruce pulled a chair over to the side of the desk, Archie turned around from the window.

"We are going to have to have a good chat about things Archie." said Bruce. Archie now leans over and supports his chin on his clasped hands.

Bruce saw a much more managerial looking man.

"Aye, we are, and I'm aware that you know little about all of this. Don't worry, ill support you and help you formulate a plan." He opened a drawer, taking out a conveniently placed pad with a pen pushed through the curved metal wire at the top. He opened the pad, scrolling for a fresh page.

"We are going to need, staff, suppliers, but most of all, customers. If there's no trade, there's no money and you'll hit a deficit very quickly."

Bruce noted that he used the word 'we not 'you.'

"A big question Archie, I can see you have put a lot of work into this place. How long would it take to get it all ready for re-opening?"

Archie leans back into the chair, blowing a long sigh through his chapped looking lips. "She's not far off, you can say a month to touch up the decorating. I'd say while that's going on, the house keeping needs to get going." He opens another drawer, this time revealing a large calculator, the sort that looks as big as an A4 bit of paper. Once again, seemingly on automatic. He starts to punch in a few figures.

"Housekeeping?" asked Bruce.

"Aye, there are 36 rooms, several communal areas, function suites, the main bar blah blah. These all need made up, the beds, bar stocked etc."

"I see, it's not straight forward, or cheap," said Bruce.

"No, far from, and you need to consider receptionists, bar and waiting staff, but above all a GM." Archie is still punching out numbers, scribbling info onto the pad.

"What's a GM?" asked Bruce.

"That is the General manager, the boss of the place. Or that can be you, the proprietor." Bruce has a feeling of worry setting in. He wasn't looking forward to the figures that were being scribbled on the pad. Archie stops writing. "Ok, we are looking at a start-up cost of, aroond 40k, that's for a month's wages for staff, food for the restaurant, booze for the bar and not least, your running costs and overheads," he announces.

Bruce shifts in his chair, absorbing the large amounts of money just mentioned. "Overheads?" he asks.

"Aye, your bills, heating, gas, electric, water, these are the main ones."

Bruce calculates the cost, taking some relief that he has the inheritance money, plus 40k of his own from investments. With the two combined, there was plenty in the kitty.

"Don't worry, the hotel will get busy, and all of these costs should be recouped monthly. She is a great money spinner in a great seaside town," said Archie. The feeling of being out of his depth intensified.

Out of the blue comes a loud bang, emanating from the reception lobby area. The two men freeze and look around

"Holy bollocks, what was that?" said Bruce. Archie didn't say a word but left his seat and walked over to the door. He grabbed the handle, pulling the door inwards and left the room. Bruce sat still, wondering what to do.

"BRUCE!" called Archie. He jumped up and quickly made his way over to the door, gripping the handle. He pulled on it hard, but the door stayed closed. Gripping it tighter, he tried again, the door handle not budging.

"ARCHIE, THE DOOR ITS STUCK," he cries out. A bead of sweat started to form on his forehead, his heart beating faster. Still no reply from the lobby. He pulled harder on the handle still.

"ARCHIE!" he cries out...no reply. Behind him, he hears a strange sound. In the panic from rattling the door, he hears an audible whisper. He didn't dare to look around as it seemed to come closer. The whisper, very human but he couldn't make out the words. His heart thumped harder, his hands sweating, the whispers right behind him...

Suddenly. "Bruce, wake up, what's going on?" asks Archie.

His eyes open slowly; he's sat with his back to the office wall. He feels cool water dripping off his forehead.

"Where am I... what happened?" he asks. Archie is still applying cool water to his head from a bowl of water and a sponge from the kitchen.

"You must have feinted, it's alright, I have got you, keep still," said Archie, offering some reassurance. Bruce is calm, feeling a bit cooler and confused. He tried to stand up, albeit a bit on the shaky side. Archie helped him into the big office chair.

"You left me Archie, and I called after you called me."

"I did call you, but I went up to the first-floor corridor, expecting you to follow."

"Why were you up there, was it the noise we heard?"

"Aye, it was, a large picture fell off the wall, just above reception," he replied.

"I tried to get out, the door, it stayed closed and the...."

"And what?" asks Archie. Bruce tilts his head back, shaking off the beads of water, rubbing his face with both hands.

"The whispers, they came at me from behind, from here!"

Archie stood up, placing the sponge in the bowl, saying nothing.

"That experience, it was terrifying, I must have passed out."

Archie made his way to the door again; he stopped and turned to face Bruce. "What do you think you heard?" he asks.

"The whispering, it was quiet at first, then loud, it got louder. Not gonna deny this, I shit myself."

"Aye, you did, and you feinted too."

"You wait there, don't you go off again, leaving me here." Bruce managed to get to his feet, suddenly feeling a bit lightheaded.

"Come on, you'll be fine, let's go and get a drink," said Archie.

They leave the office, on the way through, Bruce touches the door and handle, feeling it in his hand. Upon inspection whilst pulling the handle up and down, the latch seemed perfectly fine, popping in and out as they should. Passing the reception counter and out into the main lobby, Bruce noticed a large picture frame with a glass cover, at least three feet across and a couple of feet tall. It was laid up against the wall opposite. The glass was shattered. He noted a couple of people on the picture. He went over to inspect it further. Without warning, a hand was placed on his right shoulder from behind.

"FOR FUCKS SAKE!" he shouts out, jumping at the same time.

"Oh, apologies Bruce, the picture, that's your auntie and uncle. It fell off the hook upstairs, pity, it was a nice image."

"They look happy in the picture," said Bruce. The picture had been blown up to this size, from an actual photo taken just after the initial completion of Dunella's refurbishment. They were both standing arm in arm, in front of the main front doors. Bruce noted that there was a large sign to the left of the entrance, now missing: 'Welcome to Dunella'

"God bless their souls," said Archie. He headed off to the kitchens. As yet that part of the hotel had not been visited. They were off to the left, of the reception entrance, at the end of a corridor, just a bit further on from the ladies and gent's toilets. As per the pattern of the day, Bruce followed his host, struggling to keep up. At the end of the corridor, was a pair of double swing-doors. Bruce sped up a little as he saw Archie push them apart and disappeared inside. Bruce almost skipped his way through. Inside the kitchen, Bruce stood just inside the double doors. He could see all the usual equipment associated with a busy kitchen. There were three aisles. On the left was a long counter, dissected by two floor-to ceiling silver fridge freezers, heading to the far end of the room. On the right, another, with a pair of ovens and gas hobs. In the centre, a wider worktop, adorned with machines of all types, a ham slicing machine and another set of electric rings. There was an odour in the air, a smell of rotten eggs. Archie was opening an internal cupboard door.

"Oh, that's another one to add to the list Bruce," he said.

"What's that then?"

"A chef." He opened the door and stepped inside; Bruce heard a clatter and a switch going on. He went over for a nosey.

"You alright Archie?"

"Aye, all good, there we are," he replied. He hands Bruce a bottle of bleach. The smell was coming from sinks at the far end, like rotten eggs. Bruce went to the far end and poured a decent amount of bleach into each of three sinks. The fluid gurgled around the plugholes. Archie opened both fridge doors. Another unpleasant smell whooshed out. He pulled out a couple of Highland Spring water bottles, checking the best before dates.

"Here Bruce, get that down you, all's ok, the dates are fine."

Bruce took the bottle and drank the whole bottle down, releasing a small burp immediately after.

"Bloody hell man, sparkling!" he blurted out, stifling another burp.

"Aye, its water all the same, you feinted, you need plenty of fluids," said Archie. Bruce started to feel better and didn't argue the point. Archie closed the door behind him and walked to the end to the right of the three sinks.

"Right Bruce, we can pop through here to the back stairwell. It's time to introduce you to your private rooms." There was a clatter from the double door end of the kitchen. Bruce briefly looked around and saw nothing.

"Wait for me please!" he said, hurrying up his pace. Archie opened the door to the stairs. Inside, there was a narrow stairwell, a winding staircase. Archie started to work his way up after getting the lighting on. The stairwell was completely stone built. The walls were medium grey blocks, with arrow slit type openings on the outside wall. The steps were solid granite. As they went up further, clutching onto a hazy brass rail, Bruce noted signage pointing to the stairs and in recesses in the wall, pairs of fire extinguishers.

"So, this is the fire escape Archie?"

"Aye, the rear stairs, known as the whining steps!"

"Did I just hear that right, whining?"

"Aye, the wind gets up and the wee arrow slits make a creepy high-pitched whine," said Archie. That was just another reason to creep Bruce out further. They pass a door to the first floor and keep on upwards. Soon they reach a small wooden door at the top, with $2^{nd}$ floor engraved on a neat brass plaque. Archie pulls out his bunch of keys. He tried a couple of keys in the lock. No luck, he tried another. Bruce could hear a feint whistle; he thought he must be imagining it as Archie had only just mentioned it. The sound became louder; the wind must have been picking up outside. Louder still, a whistling whine. He looked around and downward. He could feel his heartbeat raising again. Then: "There we go, finally," announced Archie.

Bruce placed a hand onto Archie's back.

"Hurry it up."

They enter a corridor. It was well lit from the main lighting. The corridor was quite long, with just a solid light pine door at each side and one right at the end. The walls were a brightly painted white and seemed a bit clinical compared to the rest of the hotel. The corridor was void of windows but there were two sky light Velux type windows sloping down to the left. Archie reached the front door. There was a Welcome mat on the pine boarded floor. First impressions were, that this was modern compared to the hotel as a whole.

"Let's see if I have better luck this time," said Archie as he slotted another key into the lock.

"There we go, all good this time," he said and entered the room.

Bruce followed him in, closing the door behind.

"Wow! I had never imagined this," said Bruce.

"Aye, it's a fine pad this one, you've been spoiled for sure."

The hallway was a large square with a single part glazed door on each wall, either side and directly in front. The floor was a dark solid reddish-brown Mahogany, varnished to a deep shine. The walls were painted a comforting pastel yellow, with a few family pictures here and there. Archie opened a small cupboard, tall and narrow, nestled in on the right-hand side of the entrance door. With his now military style application, he flicked up the main fuses on the fuse board.

"There, should all be on now, I hope to hell they emptied the fridge/freezer," he joked.

"Well so far, I can't smell rotten eggs like we did in the kitchens," remarked Bruce. Archie opened the door to the right and stepped inside, Bruce followed closely. "Wow! I wasn't expecting this, Archie."

The door opened up into a large lounge, with a long picture window in front of them, looking out to the very rear of the grounds. From this height it was an exceptional view. Bruce stood at the window admiring the view. He was a bit gob-smacked to say the least. The decor was immaculate. The walls were that light pastel yellow, with just one that was a feature wall; a nice light blue. On that wall was a posh set up of TV units and drawer units. They were a dark wood and glistened in the light. There was a fancy sofa, long enough to seat four and two complimenting armchairs. These were a nice cream leather, spotless and 'as new.'

Archie took a seat. "So comfy these, you'll have a super place to retreat to Bruce." He joined him and sat in the middle of the large sofa, musing out at the view. "I can't believe this, why did the agent not show this off?"

"I can only assume they were busy, Cindy I mean, they are always overworked, the property market is booming in the Ferry the noo," he replied in his usual broad Scots accent.

"You have a dining room through the door to the right, as we walked into the lobby. It adjoins via the kitchen just through there. There are two double bedrooms up here too." Archie stood up and made his way to the door at the far end of the room.

"Lovely, no smell so far," he said as he entered the kitchen. Bruce followed him in and was keen to see the layout. It didn't disappoint. The units were a nice white colour, spread around the walls, in a square shaped room. In the centre was a nice central isle, all were accented with beautiful slate-coloured solid worktops. There was a modern looking Aga type oven, with huge gas rings. It was superb. There was one window on the left, looking out over the grounds, set just above the sink and draining board. Just to add a bit of status to the sink, were a set of gold-plated Victorian style taps. Archie disappeared through another door at the other side of the kitchen. Bruce didn't want him to go again so he hurried after him.

"Where you off to now?" he called out

"This doorway leads to the adjacent corridor with the bedrooms," said Archie. Indeed, another corridor, and yes two more doors on the left-hand side. The corridor was exactly the same as the entrance lobby, in regard to the decor. A welcoming clean pastel yellow and spotless. This time, there was a carpet, a nice light brown short pile, commonly called 'seagrass'

They headed through the first door into the bedroom.

"Fabulous, just like the rest of it up here," said Bruce.

"Aye, not much spared up here. Your predecessors went to town."

They did exactly that. This room was a bit different. The walls were papered, a nice pattern, flowered all colours, but Scottish thistle here and there. Very bright, and modern. Bruce didn't know too much about his uncle's previous involvement with the building industry. He knew next to nothing about the skills Uncle Stanley had acquired over the years, and running DMS, his maintenance company. Archie pulled the curtains open a bit further, revealing another nice view. This time it was the side of Dunella, facing an adjacent road, just off the main Albany Road. Archie opened a door in the centre of the bedroom, revealing the bathroom. The room was roomy and had a sun pipe bringing light in from above. Bruce wanted a peek. He wasn't disappointed. There was a fancy bath suite, marble tiled with gold inlaid strips running from the marble floor to ceiling. A stand -in shower, similar scheme and a wide basin, with a huge mirror. Like the kitchen, the taps and even the shower head were gold plate.

"I'm blown away with all this, it's amazing in here," said Bruce.

"Your uncle, he was a dab hand at most things. He put an awful lot of money into this space; you should have seen it before he put his mark on it."

"So, what did he do before the hotel?"

"He owned Dundee Maintenance Services. (DMS) as they were known. Back in the 80's he coined it in, mainly because so many trades were working abroad in Germany specifically. They sold the company, tax debts as far as I know," said Archie, now taking a quick pee in the toilet.

"Tax debts, ewww, sounds bad," replied Bruce.

Archie finished up and flushed the loo, thankfully it worked. He lifted the back of the cistern cover off, making sure the water side inlet valve was functioning properly.

"So, they had to sell DMS, due to bad debts?" asks Bruce.

"Aye, they had a dodgy account firm, meddling the books, your uncle was an honest man, a great businessman. That's why they did so well here."

"How did they afford Dunella then?"

"A German investor, he bought out DMS and the money at the time covered the debts, bought this and left plenty over for the refurb work."

Archie pulled the bathroom door closed and headed out to the corridor. They had a brief look in the 2nd room, and it was almost identical. The only difference was that there was a shower in the corner, built inside a small room, with just a toilet and wash basin. This was probably the room intended for guests and wasn't nearly so extravagant. Eventually they made their way around to the door that was opposite the front door. This was the corridor to the bedrooms. There was a final door to explore, the one to the right of the front door. This one was locked. Out came the key bunch.

"Hmmm, bit on the stiff side this one," said Archie, struggling with the lock mechanism. He persists and it clunked open. In they went and were welcomed with a very different room this time. The walls were panelled in wood from floor to about midway. A dark stained Oak colour. The upper wall all the way around was a mirror. The floor was similarly laid in oak and the table in the middle of the room had a fabulous shine, with a set of six chairs neatly tucked in. To the right was another picture window, this time looking out over the front of Dunella. The feeling here was a relaxed dining room, a family room. In the middle of the table was a silver set of trays with a couple of candle holders, supporting a couple of tall red candles. One of the focal points was a beautiful medium sized chandelier, shining brightly, projecting colourful images on the walls. The focal point in here was the fireplace. This took his breath away. On the other side of the room was a stone-built fireplace. It was a good couple of metres wide with an ornamental solid stone mantel piece. The fire was open and clearly designed for coal.

"Ah, the thing of beauty right there," said Archie.

"It is indeed, I love it, does it work?" replied Bruce.

I'll show you; it's not coal, it's a fake version of it. The fire is gas."

Archie shuffled over to the fireplace. Up on the hearth was a small tin box, with a box of matches inside.

"Here we go, I'll just turn this knob," he knelt down and turned a small brass knob, the sound of gas very evident. And then he struck a match, placing it into the base of the fire.

'WOOSH.' crackle and pop. The fire exploded into life. The heat from the flames suddenly warming the room, immediately taking the chill away.

Bruce couldn't resist any more and pulled out a chair, staring into the flames. Archie joined him, scraping the floor as he did. They sat still, looking into the fire as it started to rapidly warm up the room. Archie laid the bunch of keys on the table. The staring lingered a little longer, both mesmerised by the fine view of flames. The tour of the hotel had taken its toll on both men, and this rest was a welcome relief. The anxiety Bruce experienced after hearing the whispering and the whining seemed to dissipate. He had a few more questions to ask. The whispers, the shadow figure in the window after the viewing with Cindy? The stuff talked about with the man who picked up his mother's settee, regarding the spiritualist church? Not to mention the lock on room 19.

"Right then Bruce, I'll be honest, I think for today I've introduced you to the works here, more or less."

"Yes, you have and I'm very grateful for your time today. There's a couple of things bothering me a bit."

"And they are?" asks Archie.

"There are a few things, I'll be honest. The whispering didn't help today, the things I've heard about Auntie Alice and a spiritualist church, oh not to mention a creepy image I saw up at a window." He looked at Archie, who leaned back into the chair, crossing his arms. He let out a long sigh, blowing his cheeks outwardly in the process. There was no response for an uncomfortable moment or two. But then: " Dunella has a few secrets, such as the cells beneath you didna know aboot. There is a long history within these walls, it's not all horrible, but it's not all good either," explained Archie. Bruce said nothing, waiting for further information.

"Some old buildings are like a recording of the past. Some say that the old building blocks somehow, regain images and memories. Ghosts if you like."

"Ghosts?"

"Aye, the scary types, you know, from folklore, legend oh and stupid films," he said. Archie was still looking into the fire, his aged face relaxed but showing signs of worry.

"Are there ghosts here?"

"Like I said Bruce, sometimes things are interpreted as such, not fully understood."

"Riddles, riddles, look do you mean this place is haunted?"

"Look Bruce, I don't want to frighten you or put a stain on your new home and business." Archie wasn't saying too much, causing an anger to rise up inside Bruce.

"For God's sake man, spit it out! Is she, or isn't she?"

"What....haunted?"

"Yes, bloody haunted." Archie looked at him, obviously a bit rattled to see him angry. But he felt he owed the new owner an honest opinion.

"I....I've seen, and I've heard strange things here. Things I can't explain. Before we go today, I'll introduce you to one more room, but it's getting late, I'd rather not be in it for too long. Bruce had a gut feeling that he knew what room was next and asked him. Archie confirmed, it was room 19. Archie got up and turned off the fire, grabbing his keys on the way to the door. They left the private suite the way they left it, if not a bit warmer than it was. This time, they exited through the front door, but just to the right was another one. At first glance it looked just like a storage cupboard. This one, already unlocked led to another corridor, this leading to the main staircase. Bruce wondered how he'd ever get used to all the routes, corridors, stairs etc. He followed as usual, passing a few more doors. He recalled Cindy telling him that there were a couple of larger rooms up there, bridal suites to name but a couple. Archie made his way down, from the $2^{nd}$ floor and onto the $1^{st}$.

A few moments later, they had reached the only room in the corridor with a hasp and staple and a shiny brass padlock on the entrance door. It was room 19. Bruce stood just behind Archie as he rattled his key bunch. The corridor seemed much gloomier than the one they had just been through. There was also a chill in the air. Archie placed a small silver key into the padlock and turned it. The lock snapped open. He took the skeleton key and placed it in the lock. He started to turn it. Then, he stopped. He said nothing, Bruce likewise. His hand holding the key starting to shake a bit.

"Are you alright?" asked Bruce.

"Absolutely fine thank you, why do you ask?"

"Oh, I noticed your hand started to shake a little, just making sure."

He stopped for a moment and looked around at Bruce.

"Just bear in mind, I had little to do in this room, it was your auntie's business what went on in here!" He turned the key and pushed open the door. They were met with a musty smell, an overpowering odour. It was a combination of the usual stale air, mixed with a slight eggy smell. Bruce could see Archie fiddling around in the dark, searching for a light switch.

"Bloody switch is knackered, hold on a wee minute," he said. Bruce waited at the entrance to the room, not exactly eager to go in. The room was pitch black.

"All ok in there Archie?" called Bruce. No answer. He called louder this time. "ARCHIE!" Still nothing. And then: "Aye, hang on a minute," he replied. Bruce looked around, he swore he heard something, like a footstep, just a bit further down the corridor. He stared at the source of the sound. The only sound yet again, was his heart pumping as his blood pressure started to raise once more. Thump......another sound, slightly closer.

"Archie, I'm coming in!" he stepped into the room, met with darkness.

"Righteo, flick on the switch on your left now." Bruce felt for the switch.

"Got it...thank goodness for that," he said as the lights went on.

"Great, the fuse had tripped in a cupboard just through in the main room," said Archie. This room was much larger than the ones Cindy had shown him around. It was one set aside for larger families or the brides. The lobby had three doors, a strange turquoise colour. The carpet was black, an odd colour Bruce thought. The walls were a pale pinkish colour. Archie had gone through the door on the right, whilst Bruce wanted to nosey in the door to the left. He opened the door, reaching in for a pull chord. The light went on revealing a nice bathroom suite, a good size, not as fancy as the private suite, he'd just been in. The bathroom suite wasn't especially fancy, white with greenish tiles and a nice, grey slate tiled floor.

   Suddenly: "BRUCE QUICKLY!" It was Archie, calling in a panic.

He headed into the other room that Archie was in. What he saw was both a shock and a bit humorous. Archie was stood struggling with a long curtain pole that had decided to come off the wall at one end.

"Bloody pole, I never knew this was just sitting there, not fixed in well at all," he said. Bruce hurried over to the far end of the room to help him.

"Oh, my goodness, here, hand me the pole end," said Bruce. He wasn't sure whether to laugh or cry at that point.

"What happened Archie?"

"I was letting in the light, the 'flaming' curtains were drawn. That's another one to add to my list of things to do." Bruce reached up and placed the pole onto the support. The curtains were open but by now it was pretty much dark outside. They had been there a good while. Archie opened a side window to let some air in. This room was large but oddly had nothing in it. No furniture, no seating, the walls bare. The annoying pale pink theme continued, a stark contrast with the black carpet.

"What's going on here then?" Bruce asks. Archie is still fiddling with the curtains. "What do you mean?"

"Well, there's no furniture, the decor is odd, black carpets to name but one." Archie made his way back to the entrance lobby.

"Follow on, the main room will help me to explain this," he said.

He got to the third door in the entrance lobby, as yet unopened. He grabbed the round brass knob, and the door opened inward.

"Hang on, wait up," said Bruce. He followed him inside. This room was enormous compared to the one they had just been in. It was at least twice the size. The exact same decor, pale pink walls, black carpet, and long curtains, still drawn way over at the opposite side. The most notable thing in this room, was the large round table, exactly placed in the middle of the room. There were two comfortable looking armchairs, one at either side of the room, facing in toward the table. Bruce felt the wooden surface, a beautiful mid brown colour, with inlaid patterns. The patterns seemed familiar, but he didn't know why. There were ornamental matching dining chairs around the table, twelve in all. Like the first room, no pictures on the walls, nothing else, just this table and chairs. He did notice the selection of candles laying on the table, just by the centre. There were about ten in all, white, red and black ones. There were three ornate looking candle holders, made from a twisted type of grey pewter or perhaps a silver plate. The only lights in the room were a single ceiling lamp at each end of the room. One was just a few feet back from the window, the other at the opposite end, by the door to the room. There was nothing above the table, just the ceiling, a dirty white unremarkable Artex.

"Well now, this is different, creepy too," said Bruce. Archie sat in an armchair. Bruce started to pull a dining chair out.

"Hold on! no, I don't think you should sit there," said Archie. Bruce pushed the chair back in.

"Why not?"

"It's not wise, look take the other seat, there's a few things I'd like to share with you." Bruce obliged and moved around the table, taking another welcome seat. He stared across the table at Bruce, waiting for him to tell him another strange story. The room was gloomy, the two ceiling lights were a low wattage. From where Bruce was sat, his buddy across the room looked more like a silhouette. Bruce had to squint at one point just to be sure it was him.

There was a stone-cold silence in the room. Both men were comfortable in their seats, but uncomfortable in mind. Bruce was starting to feel a bit chilly too and noted that there wasn't a fireplace in the room, not even a radiator. Only the circular table, twelve dining chairs, two armchairs and the assembly of candles. The only sound, a quiet whistle as the wind outside blew against the window.

"Well, Archie, this is different, what's going on here?"

Archie remained quiet, his silhouette still. "Archie?" asked Bruce.

"Aye, sorry I almost nodded off in this seat. It's not a case of 'what's going on,' more like what went on?" he said.

"What do you mean by that?"

"Bruce, I don't know that much, I wasn't involved, you'll be pleased to know, but I've been here long enough to overhear conversations and pick up on certain vibes."

"Vibes?" asks Bruce. He shifts in his chair. Archie fell silent once again.

"I think you should know things, you are the new owner, I don't want to freak you out and make you feel uncomfortable."

"Archie, it's really a bit late for that, this place has been creeping me out more or less since we got here today."

He could see Archie nodding his head, as if he was in agreement that more information should be shared. The outside wind was increasing in strength. The whistle intensified in the quietness of the room.

"That noise isn't exactly helping," said Bruce. One of the two ceiling lights flickered on and off, adding to the creepy atmosphere.

"Ok, I'll share this with you, but remember some things should stay quiet, secret, between us......understood?" said Archie.

"Fire away." Bruce was all ears as he kept looking to the draughty window. There are a few things linked with this very room, and they are not all good. There is a rumour that a horrific incident took place right here." he said. Bruce let out a nervous hum sound, as that information filtered through. "Oh, what was horrific?"

"Murder, the taking of a young life, in this room!" announced Archie.

Bruce placed a hand over his chin, his eyes switching from the silhouette to the whistly window. He experienced a wave of shivers up and down the back of his neck.

"Shit!" said Bruce. He senses his heart increasing in pace once again, a theme of the evening. The lid was lifted off the can of worms now. Archie had made a statement; a profound bit of information. Many old buildings are awash with rumour and local legend. Whiskey was often the fuel behind ghost sightings in Scotland, especially that of the Loch Ness Monster. He wanted to know more about Dunella. He wanted the truth, but at the same time, he felt an apprehension about knowing more. The flickering ceiling lamp of two finally gave up, making a popping sound as the light went out.

"Holy, bum heads!" said Bruce. He looked up at the light and over to the silhouette of Archie. He got up and rattled about in his jacket pocket, revealing a gas lighter.

"What are you doing now?" asked Bruce.

"I'm going to light a candle or two, seems appropriate now we have a light doon." He picked up a red coloured candle and placed it into one of the holders. He struck the lighter filament and lit the candle. Sitting back down, Bruce noted that Archie's silhouette was now a bit creepier than before. His face seemed to go in and out of focus as the light flickering from the candle, created a mix of shadow and light around the room.

"Well, this isn't creepy, right Archie?"

"Och, no, this is nice and calm, you need to relax Mr Gordon. I am about to elaborate on what we touched upon earlier."

"I won't beat about the bush, the incident that took place in here. That's shrouded in mystery. It was the war years, and a lot of death was going on, not just here, but everywhere," he said. He got up briefly to check the blown ceiling lamp, tapping it a few times, but it stayed off. He sat back down and continued further.

"It was a crime of passion, one of the owners from that ear. He fell in love with a much younger woman. She was a bit promiscuous and in a jealous rage; the owner put an end to her affair."

"Put an end to it, how?" asks Bruce.

"It is said he waited in here, until things got hot and steamy, then he calmly revealed an axe, his weapon of choice. The rest is history."

"Right here?" asks Bruce.

"Right here, this was a bedroom then, now it's changed around a bit."

Well, that's a little chilling, if it actually happened," said Bruce.

"I'm told it did happen, and there was a bit of a cover-up at the time, there's not too much about it on record."

"Oh, why the cover up?"

"One of the victims, the Canadian, he was a high-ranking officer in the army. At that time, certain things were not exactly sung from the rooftops," said Archie. Bruce surprisingly wasn't too terrorised at this story, perhaps due to the passage of time. He wanted to know more.

"And the so-called owner, what happened to him?" he asks.

"I only know that he was a bit of a mysterious character. I have heard through the grapevine that he committed suicide," said Archie. Bruce obviously wanted to know where that happened. Little did he know that the suicide took place from hie private quarters, when Tobias leapt from a window, crashing to the ground, putting an end to his unsettled life.

"I had heard it may have taken place within the hotel, but I don't know where or how it was done," explained Archie. He actually did know about it, more than he explained. For now, he felt it unsavoury to part with such detail. That would certainly make for an uncomfortable experience for Bruce as he was soon to move into the very suite where it took place.

"Ok, I hear you Archie, all this hearsay and stories, they are commonplace in such old places. What is the connection with this odd layout in here?" Archie sat forward, looking directly at the candle.

"The last owner, your aunt, she was involved with a spiritualist church, and she had a particular gift."

"The Church, would that be the Bon-Accord?"

"Aye, it's a popular one, a spiritualist church," said Archie, he looked surprised that Bruce knew about it.

"How did you hear about that then?"

"I was clearing out my mother's house and a friend of Alice collected a settee. He knew auntie and about the church."

"Your mothers place, so she also got involved in the church?" asked Archie.

"Yes, for a while, she found comfort there after my dad died, according to Jack, aunties friend."

"I suppose they were close then, your mum and Alice?"

"I guess, why?"

"Oh, nothing, nothing to worry about," said Archie. Bruce checked his watch and saw that it was close to nine. Time was ticking by; they had been at the hotel for almost three hours. Bruce mentioned the time and that he needed to head home soon. He was also sure that the information he'd heard from Archie wasn't quite over. He wanted to find out just a little more before heading off.

"This room, the table, the lack of things, is there a connection to this church and the gift my auntie had?"

"Aye, look, don't be alarmed, it was more or less a hobby of hers," replied Archie.

"Hobby....what doing?"

"She used to hold séances in this place, at this table." He stood up, he felt it was time to go and had heard enough. He walked over to the window, peering through at the dark night. The wind had dropped, and the room seemed like the quietest place on earth.

"Oh great, is that when people apparently contact the dead, that's just all Gobbledegook, right?" Archie stepped over to the candle, blowing it out and looked directly at him and said:

"Aye, maybe.... maybe not!"

"So, this room, it's not being used for paying guests, clearly?" asked Bruce. Archie placed the part burned candle with the others, methodically tidying them up. "That is the case, she was very involved in this stuff. There were all sorts of people coming and going here, in hope to contact departed loved ones."

"That's all nonsense, we'll be getting this room back in order, and wipe that nonsense away for good!"

# Chapter seven

They finally left room 19 and stood outside. Archie carefully replaced the padlock, pulling on it a couple of times to make sure it was locked.

"What exactly are you locking in there?" asks Bruce.

"Oh, nothing, you saw for yourself, its bare."

They headed off along the corridor, back down the grand staircase to reception. Archie went back into the office, placing the keys in the safe. Bruce had been holding it in for a while, reluctant to use number 19's toilet. So, he popped into the gents. He thought he heard a sound as he opened the entrance door. There were two out of the three sinks running. He touched the water on one of them and could feel that the water was warm, signalling that the gas was working fine. He turned them off and peered at himself briefly through the cracked mirror, he'd notice on the first viewing.

'Gobbledegook' he thought and used the urinal.

"BRUCE!" called Archie. He finished up, if a little messy due to the interruption. "YES, JUST IN THE GENTS!"

He needed to wash his hands now and stepped around to the sinks. The two that he had just shut off were running. He stopped and stared at them, daring not to move. "ARCHIE!" he calls out. Moments later he enters the toilet. "What's a matter?" he asks.

"These sinks, the taps, they were on, I turned them off, then they came on again." Archie turned them off, then back on.

"I think you're a wee bit tired Mr Gordon, their fine, it's time to head off." Leaving the gents, Bruce certainly had been given a much better insight into the hotel. Most of it was great and he was happy. Room 19 didn't exactly help on top of a couple of other experiences that bothered him. Archie shut off the main lighting, but decided on keeping the reception area light on, for additional security. They talked briefly again about timings and when Bruce would move in. It was decided that another meeting would have to take place before that happened. The business plan, staffing, finance etc. was all a very real and a serious aspect to it all. Archie was obviously a key factor to all of that. In many ways, Bruce was relieved he was involved. They walked to the entrance lobby and Archie pulled the double inner doors closed.

"Right Bruce, there's no time like the present. I'm going to exit first, and you will set the alarm." He handed a piece of paper over with a small instruction on it:

```
To set alarm:
Press centre arrow key twice
Press pin numbers 33781
Press enter
There is a 15 second arm time
```

Archie left the building and watched closely as he punched in the numbers.
As expected, the countdown bleeps were sounded, and Bruce rushed his way out. They stood outside and waited for the bleeping to stop.
"Well done, all set, she's in safe hands the now," said Archie.
"Thanks, guess I need to get used to it."
"There's going to be an awful lot to get used to here Bruce, you won't master any of it overnight."
It was pretty dark outside by now and the temperature had dropped significantly. They breathed in the cool night air, admiring the moon light illuminating the front grounds. They spoke for a couple more minutes while Archie fiddled about with his bicycle. It was decided that they would meet at the weekend, in a cafe in the ferry. Archie headed off on his bike, leaving Bruce to head to his car alone. He hurried up and dropped the keys in the process. In the moon light he could just see the glint of metal and thought he'd

found them. It was a ring pull. He pulled his mobile out and selected the torch and started to scour the gravel for the keys.

"Where the bollocks are you!" he said in the gloom. He started to panic again, aware that he was alone this time. There wasn't a sound, not a soul around, the wind had died right down. He dropped to his hands and knees.

"Bloody hell, where the!" he keeps swiping his hands from left to right, the cool gravel dampening his knees. From behind him, he hears a footstep, then another, the gravel parting unmistakably. The sound getting closer and closer still. He looks around, still sifting the gravel. There's nothing, nobody, no fox, just the dead quiet darkness. Another step, Bruce can see the welcoming streetlamps and thinks about running to the roadside.

'Calm yourself down' he thinks, the voice in his head so familiar from dodgy situations experienced with the military. Louder they get, he's met with a sudden gust of ice-cold wind. And then he shouts out in relief:

"THANK CHRIST FOR THAT!"

He found the keys, and darts over to his car. The cool wind seemed to follow him. He presses the key fob and the door opens. In his panicky state trying to put the key in the ignition, he drops the keys into the foot well. "SHIT!" he cries out, fiddling between his shoes for the keys in the darkness. He cries out again:

"COME ON YOU...."

He locates the keys and finally gets the car started up, proceeding to rev the engine. Suddenly and absolutely not welcomed at this point, a knock on the driver's window. He eased off the pedal and in a state of terror looks out.

"Oh my...f... what are you doing back here?" he said, it was Archie.

He winds the window down.

"Are you ok Bruce, have you got a bit of engine trouble?"

"Archie no, all's fine, just dropped my keys and got a bit spooked."

"Ah, I see, look, pleased I caught you, my mobile has decided to pack up, and I just wanted to say, meet at 12pm this Saturday at Visocchi's in the town. They do a nice brunch, my treat ok?"

"Great I'll see you there, you take care now in the wind on that bike."

"Don't, worry aboot me, bye now, oh and next time you are here, relax!" A relieved Bruce started the journey home. He was happy on the whole with the evening at Dunella. The place is certainly mysterious with plenty of history. He wasn't prepared for discovering that she had been built upon a former early prison. He hadn't prepared himself either for the stories of murder, suicide and 'contacting the dead!' He started to think about the plan that he would put together with Archie, reminding himself that he was key to so much in the hotel. He kept on thinking about the whisper, the unexplained sound heard in the office. To add to the mix, the whining sounds on the rear stairwell. The taps in the gents refusing to stay off. But, on the whole, he was happy and still excited about what he was now a part of. To be a proud new owner of a hotel and to be able to finally close the door on the army, more than outweighed his recent experiences. If ever he had been in an old building as man and boy, they always have a story, an atmosphere and a history of good and bad events. He put all of his experiences in a 'normal' box at the back of his mind. The rest of the week would be a 'winding down' at work few days. There was less than a month left to serve before he discharged with a full month's holiday owed.

He had a great deal to sort out with the hotel. Anything done at work now, would pale into insignificance. Everything he got involved with from now on would be taken with a pinch of salt. The biggest worry on his mind at the moment, was moving into Dunella. Giving up his military home of many years and moving into a huge hotel, there's no comparison. For a time, as yet uncertain, he would be alone at the hotel, another uncomfortable thought. The sooner guests arrive the better.

The next morning, he got up as usual, washed and shaved, dressed up in his uniform, made a bowl of porridge for breakfast and put on the kettle. This was more or less the same pattern for many years. He sat at the kitchen table, listening to radio 4. Slurping on his hot coffee, absorbing the news announcement. Another three British deaths in Helmand Province. That year, 2008, was one of the toughest for the coalition. The operation had switched from taking the Taliban on directly, to concentrating on defeating the insurgency. The strength of the Taleban had been weakened massively, and they withdrew to the mountainous regions. What remained were pockets of resistance that mounted a vicious assault on troops from all nations involved. The main threats were from the notorious IED munitions.

An IED, short for Improvised Explosive Device, was exactly what it said on the tin. These were not pretty, make-shift bombs and mines. They were skilfully assembled literally in the equivalent of a shed or a garage. That made detection virtually impossible. It didn't take much for a knowledgeable elder who may have been trained by the American army or CIA during the Soviet era, to teach a group of men of all ages and back grounds. A typical example could be as simple as a metal ammunition box, plentiful in the country, filled with explosive and connected to a wire of a required length. Later, the insurgents used wooden boxes as they couldn't easily be detected by a MD8, sometimes nicknamed 'Valance.' This was a vital military version of a metal detector. This would then be placed virtually anywhere it was required. Usually at a road junction or under a water culvert. They were often simply dug into the ground, set up as a land mine. These had a simple device inside that triggered when a weight, such as a vehicle drove onto it. This version claimed many lives, and this is how Bruce's best friend 'Nuts' was killed.

The radio announcement brought back a few memories. His time in Afghanistan was a mixed bag. He had a brilliant experience, doing the job he was trained to do. As a hardened battle tested soldier, it was more or less just another day at the office. However, this conflict was unlike most in so many ways. The smaller groups of insurgents were skilled in the aforementioned deadly ways. They would apply their deadly equipment with the local knowledge of the ground; a massive advantage over the coalition forces. This was a huge threat. Bruce thought about the time there and the loss of his best friend. Currently, his regiment was involved in the preparation for an upcoming British operation, due the following year, known as 'Panthers Claw'.

With this in mind, he suddenly experienced a sadness not felt for the past few weeks. The hotel and the money had blinkered his life and job within the army. This particular morning brought on a feeling of shame and guilt that he hadn't expected. The news had triggered so many memories. He turned off the radio and headed for work on his bicycle. That day, the office was more quiet than usual. Mikey had put in for leave for the next two weeks. That meant Bruce was alone, apart from the occasional bit of contact and banter with reception. The next couple of days came and went, similarly uneventful, the days filled with his typical duties. He was looking forward to meeting up with Archie again at Visocchi's in Broughty Ferry. Friday morning came and as usual, the bike ride was made, and he got to his empty office. Only today, there was a large brown A4 envelope on his desk.

He had seen so many over his time in the office, but this one clearly had his name and rank stamped across it. He made a coffee and stood at the window, staring out across the parade square he had been on so many times before, both as a private and as a drill instructor. He sat back at his desk and stared down at the envelope. He knew exactly what it was but wanted to delay touching it. For a career soldier of almost 30 years, this was a very poignant moment. It seemed like five minutes ago when he was filling in a similarly sized form at his local army careers centre as a fresh out of school sixteen-year-old. He had not planned for the emotion he was fighting back.

He tore it open and sat back in his seat. It was the official resignation acceptance that had been signed off. There was a lot of information in the letter, but cutting through the chaff, it acknowledged his service in the army and stated the official discharge date. Reading through the papers, he could feel a chilled tear wandering down a cheek. He wiped it away and came to the acknowledgement 'sign here' section. This proved tougher still. He pulled out his favourite pen, one that had been in Afghanistan with him. The point hovered over the empty box. He breathed in deeply as it touched the paper. Suddenly, he's startled as the office door is knocked.

"HELLO, COME IN," he calls. The door swings open and in steps Chloe from reception. The distraction from signing seemed a relief. He had never taken much notice of her, but today she was nicely dressed. Chloe was in her early thirties, with long blonde hair. A typical civilian receptionist working within a military establishment. She would dress to kill and was known for having a fling or two during the past few years she had worked on camp. Bruce liked her but he was always attracted to brunettes, such as Cindy the agent. However, today, Chloe was wearing an all-black business suit, her bare legs from just above the knee reaching down into a short, heeled pair of black shoes. She was sporting her usual fake eyelashes, and had lips that reminded him of a rubber doll one of the lads was found abusing on camp a few years earlier. They were certainly the same deep red colour.

"What can I do for you Chloe?" She walked in and sat on Mikey's desk. "I heard through the grape vine that a certain Staff Sergeant is leaving us," she said.

"Oh, did you now, I wonder who from?" he replied, instantly knowing it would have come from Mikey.

"Yeah, I have, and I'll be honest, it's a shock; everyone's on about it."

"Yes, I can imagine, can't keep anything a secret around here," he replied. Bruce stared at the empty signature box again, then looked up at her. "You fancy a cuppa?" She accepts, as he switches the kettle on for the fifth time already that day. He sat back with his coffee, and he mused at her as she pulled Mikey's chair out, sitting just near the end of Bruce's desk. She was close enough for him to suddenly sneeze on a certain strong perfume, the lovely scent filling the stale office air.

"So, what's with the lovely black business suit?" he asks.

"Oh, this is me at 3pm, my Aunt Doreen passed; it's her funeral day."

"Shit, sorry to hear that, I can relate to that."

"Yes, I heard all about your auntie and your bit of good fortune," she said. This time, it was all out of the bag. There was no need to hide it, and it seemed everyone knew anyway.

"Yes, I have, I'm a hotelier now," he said smiling, and in that moment, he signed the empty box and slipped the paperwork into a drawer.

"Yep, I heard all about it, you must be over the moon?"

"I am, I'm obviously sad to lose another family member, but at the same time, I'm really happy. Now I can retire from here a bit earlier too."

She slurps on her coffee like an annoying teenager, looking over her mug, fluttering her ridiculous fake eyelashes. She crossed her legs and stared at him, he noticed but looked away. The distraction from his signature was very welcomed though and came at the right time.

"So, when will the hotel open, it's been closed a while?" she asks.

"Soon as I can fix up a few things and hire enough staff and the like."

"I can be of assistance you know?" He wasn't quite sure where that comment was going and:

"How is that?"

"I'm a receptionist am I not?"

"Yes, but you work here."

"Not for too long, my civvy contract is up in a few weeks; I'll be looking for a job." He paused for a few moments, thinking about what Archie had talked about, the plan, staff and the like.

"Well, I'm keen to have you on board if you're willing?"

"Oh, I am for sure, I can run a hotel reception no problem, I have been head receptionist at The Bartholomew a few years ago." She ended that statement with another flutter of her false eyelashes. This time, he noticed, and it made him feel a bit uncomfortable. However, he was brand new at this whole game. He was a soldier, not a hotelier. He knew that like with Archie, he would have to reel it in and listen to those in the know. For many years now, he was the one giving the orders; now that had to change.

"Look, Chloe, I hear you, and I do need support with this. I'm meeting a business associate this weekend to go over all sorts of things, moving forward." She got up and leaned over his desk, another interesting moment as he tried not to look at her unique attribute.

"Right, I need to get off, pardon the pun; my number, let me know how your chat goes," she said, scribbling her number on the corner of a yellow post-it note. She left the office, leaving a strong scent behind. She threw another spanner into the works, highlighting the issue with his inexperience and lack of business sense. 'What the hell am I doing?' he thinks, rubbing his clammy hands together. He opened the drawer and took out the brown envelope. Pulling out the contents just to make certain the signature was done correctly, with nothing else missed. It was all ok and it was done. The deal was sealed, in just a couple of months, out of the blue, his life took a new path.

Saturday morning arrived. Bruce rolled out of bed at his usual 5.30am. He had five hours to go before meeting Archie for brunch. There was so much information spinning around his head that there was only one thing left for it; a morning jog. After pulling on his jogging bottoms and having a quick wash and shave, he headed for the kettle. He noted that this morning he was suffering a bad headache. Not surprising considering everything. The kettle boils, in went a double heaped spoon of coffee, and a complimentary couple of spoons of sugar. The next thing, again habitual routine, he made a small bowl of porridge. This was definitely a great fuel for a run. His birthday, May 19th, strongly put him in the Taurus arena, and these people are known for routine.

It was another drizzly morning, not very favourable for his usual running route. He was praying that if he left before seven; the chances were greatly reduced of him bumping into nosey neighbour. He leaves the front door, looking around quietly to his right for Jimmey. The coast was clear. He leaps across the road to the pathway entrance and soon relaxes into his mile from home run and back. The path was very muddy, and Bruce had to adjust his running style to avoid slipping. There had been some lads recently found racing up and down the track on mountain bikes. This was ok apart from one of them almost run Jimmey over a few weeks ago. The ruts left by the bikes had not helped the slushy uneven ground. Bruce loved this route; it had been his mainstay for exercise for as long as he'd lived in the house. As a man in his late forties, there was nothing better for keeping the heart pumping and the weight off. He didn't drink much but he was known for binge drinking with the lads from time to time. He was more of a 'social' drinker as opposed to routine. The latter a big issue in the army

The rain came down harder now. The wind increasing. He slipped at one point, causing him to stop and walk for a few metres. After about running a mile out, like so many times before, he turned at the chosen tree point, making a start on the return journey. All was well, a good pace, and then. He ran into a deeper than usual puddle, catching him off balance, causing him to slip, lunging off the pathway to the right. His head making contact with a felled tree trunk.

Everything went black. Everything went silent. He lays there to the side of the soaked and muddied pathway, still. He was temporarily knocked unconscious. He stands in darkness, with nothing around him.

'What the?' he thinks, but no sound leaves his mouth. He feels down and can feel his legs and reaches to touch his face. There is utter darkness. He senses he is all there, but where exactly? 'This is different,' he thinks. 'Am I blind...am I dead?' he asks himself again.

'Come on what's happening here?' his thoughts are confused.

"Hey!" calls a voice, not too loudly and not too far away. He looks around in the darkness, there's nothing, and nobody.

"Hey, Bruce!" the voice calls, this time a little closer. He turns around in a full 360 motion, looking out into blackness. Suddenly, there is a point of light, in the distance, creating a lit-up reflection on the ground. He looks along the reflection. It is a pathway of light. He feels calm but wonders about this sight. 'What now?' he thinks He tries to step forward but can't move.

"BRUCE!" calls the voice, louder this time. He focuses on the end of the lit pathway. There in the distance he sees the figure of a person. The figure is moving closer, but not walking, hovering, silently.

"It's me old buddy," says the voice.

"Who exactly?"

"You forgot my voice already?... nice." He thinks about the voice as the image of a person gets closer, now only a few metres away. The light from behind causing the silhouette to increase in size. The darkness on all sides and all around intensified. The illuminated path awash with pure white light. Bruce watched as the silhouette got closer still. "Any idea yet Bruce?" the voice asks. Bruce didn't know how to respond. In normal circumstances his heart would fill his mouth and pound through his chest. It suddenly clicked!

"Nathan?" he said.

"Oh, Nathan, not 'Nuts' for a change?" the silhouette said. It crept ever closer, now just a few feet in front. The silhouette stops dead in its tracks and starts to take on colour revealing a face. Bruce is still unable to move off the spot. He is still at a loss with this situation.

"Nuts......I. It can't be you, you're d," said Bruce, only just announcing the first letter, before the coloured in silhouette replied.

"Dead! Not me, just moved on." Bruce couldn't believe his eyes as the image of his dead mate took on more and more colour. He was now very much solid and very much the person that Bruce mourned over in Afghanistan.

"This is not real, you can't be real," said Bruce

"It is, I am, and I am here, same as you old pal." He moved closer still and had all the features that Bruce remembered him by. Black crewcut hair, chiselled jaw. The strange part was that the gaping wounds both to his upper neck and forehead were gone. The explosion sent molten steel chunks from underneath the vehicle they were in, upwards. One of the lethal pieces embedded itself into Nathans neck, splitting into two parts, one of which exited from his forehead causing what was left of his already smashed brain to spill out.

"Nuts held his hand out, offering a handshake. Bruce obliged and their hands came together as tightly as in reality.

"Your hand, its solid," said Bruce

"Yes, yours too pal." The handshake turned into a gentle embrace. The emotion was all over his dead comrade's face.

"Nuts, this is nuts!" said Bruce. He could feel that he was free and no longer stuck on the spot. He looked down at his feet and could see that he was wearing dark shoes, not the trainers that were so obviously white and blue, spattered in mud. Nuts also had the same type on, and he was wearing a tidy set of clothes. It seemed that they were both wearing a suit, tidy and very formal. Bruce felt relaxed, knowing that he was in the company of his long-lost best friend. But why? How?

"You were dead, your brains were all over the bloody Mastif!"

"I was, and they were, and guess what?"

"What?" asks Bruce.

"I'm still alive, albeit in a slightly different form, but I'm still me pal." This time, this situation, he had no explanation and was lost for words.

"You want to know why you are here I suppose Bruce?"

"Just a little, guess I'm dead too?" He reaches down again, rubbing his hands on his thighs, making sure he hadn't disappeared. He was very much there.

"Buddy, you are not dead yet. We never die, we just move from one place and on to the next. All the films, remember Ghost?" he asks Bruce.

"Yes, great film, but was a film though."

"It was, but very much like what happens after you leave your old body behind. When I was blown to bits I instantly sat next to the mess, me that was and I saw your reaction, could smell and hear and witness everything," explained Nuts.

"This can't be happening, it's fucked up, clearly, I'm having a bad dream." Suddenly, Nuts claps his hands together and they are both stood outside of the darkness. They are on the pathway in the rain looking at a lifeless body on the side of the path.

"That's me, what the...we...where?" asks Bruce.

They stare at the body, and in a moment, a cyclist passes straight through them both. There was no sound, no feeling of rain and no feeling at all as the cyclist passed by.

"Am I dead or what?"

"No, you are ok, a bit unconscious, you slipped and hit your head on that tree trunk." He notices a trickle of blood running down his cheek, oozing from a small gash on his head.

"Look over there," said Nuts. "That cyclist, he noticed you and he is going to come back. He helps you home and your fine, shaken, with a headache, but fine." They watch as the cyclist did indeed turn around and headed back towards them. A clap of hands and they are back in the darkness, with the illuminated path still lighting them up.

"So, if I'm not dead, what is this place and why am I here?"

"This is what people call 'The afterlife,' in layman's terms. It's the next step, we die and move to this step and then another and so on,"

"So, you are a ghost?" asks Bruce.

"No, you can feel me as I can you." Nuts slapped him on the back, and he could not only here the thud but felt the sensation.

"There's no time to explain, people come here from there and move on. Some though, take a different path," said Nuts.

"Path, how do you mean?" asks Bruce.

"When I was killed, I looked at me and you and knew what had happened, but then in an instant, I came here."

"Just here, in the darkness?" Nuts starts to laugh, reminding Bruce that he was very much his lost friend.

"You come here then, if it's your time, they come and take you to the land yonder that doorway. You know the stories, into the light, the tunnels blah bloody blah; they are all true!"

"What about the paths you were saying?"

"Yes, some who do evil things go into a state of a kind of unsettlement. They come here but linger on the periphery of the entrance. They are stuck between the old world and this one."

"Just like in the films and stuff," said Bruce.

"Yep, exactly that, and I don't make the rules; it's all a bit weird." Nuts starts to move backwards at an increasing pace. He was still facing Bruce and slowly his features became darkened again as the light turned him into silhouette.

"What now, why was I here, you didn't say?" Nuts is getting ever smaller as he moves backwards towards the light source.

"Oh, that's easy pal, Dunella, there's evil within her walls. You will have my protection, but others may not." he said

"Dunella, but how do you know about that?"

"I just do, and I said, I don't make the rules pal. You got to go now as do I; I'll be seeing you."

"NUTS, BUT......," he called out. Then in an instant.

"Hey, are you ok Mr?" asked the cyclist. Bruce woke from his moment of unconsciousness.

"Um. Yeah, all good... where am I?"

"You're laying at the side of the pathway, soaked to the bone; you must have fallen or something," said the stranger. "Here, let me help you up." He put his bike at the side of the pathway and placed his arms under his armpits. "Right, I'll lift. You just push ok," he said. He slowly gets up onto his feet.

"Are you ok Mr, you're bleeding." Bruce feels his head where the pain is focused, looking at the blood on his fingertips.

"I'm ok, I must have slipped...Nuts!"

"Who or what's nuts?" asked the man.

"Oh, that's my best friend, he was here...where is he gone?" The man holds him up and can see that Bruce is a bit disorientated. They start to head along the track and home. The man leaves his bicycle behind so he can put an arm around Bruce, offering him good support.

"What time is it?" asks Bruce.

"Oh, it's about 8.30."

"I had a strange dream back there, creepy like," said Bruce.

"You were out cold when I cycled by, I thought you were a homeless the way you were laying there in the rain," said the man.

"What's your name?" asks Bruce.

"Patrick, call me Pat."

"Pleased to meet you Pat, thanks a lot for your help." They walked further, as they did so Bruce started to feel better.

"I've not seen you on the pathway before, you must be over six feet tall, how would I ever miss you?" Pat fell silent for a few moments then replied.

"I have been on this track many times, I used to ride a fine horse too, a long time ago, until..."

"Until what?" asks Bruce. Pat didn't offer a reply.

It wasn't the first time he had been knocked out. Thirty years of fighting across the world in all sorts of situations had made sure of that. He started to think about the vision of Nuts. The whole thing seemed a bit dream-like. He wasn't sure if that had happened or was just a dream, brought on by being unconscious. He did remember the message from Nuts. That Dunella was evil or at least had something evil within. For now, he was happy to just put it behind him and needed to focus on the meeting with Archie. They reached the end of the pathway.

"Where do you live?" asked Pat.

"Well, conveniently I'm just across the road there," he replied. Pat helps him over the road to his front door. He feels a lot better, just a headache, although he had left the house with one anyway.

"Do you think you need the hospital; I can take you?" said Pat.

"No, I'm good now, I'll overdose on caffeine and a couple of paracetamols."

"Well, you have a small gash, it needs a clean, its stopped bleeding so guess you don't need a stitch. You were lucky." Bruce offered Pat a cuppa, but he needed to go. He wanted to get indoors and clean up for the meeting anyway. He fumbled with the keys and heard the front gate close, turning to say goodbye.... but: he was gone!

"What the?" he said aloud. He walks to the garden gate.

'That's impossible,' he thinks. He opens the gate and crosses over the road to look for Pat, but the pathway is clear, not a soul.

'Right, kettle, coffee, painkillers, and I need a bloody shrink!' he thinks. He looks across at the house, soon to be a memory. The coasts clear, no Jimmey, but then. Jimmey's front door opens, and he steps out onto the soaked ground with slippers on and wearing a dressing gown that really should not be seen in public.

"You alright Bruce on this shitty rainy morning?" he asks. Bruce calms his head and was about to exchange an expletive, army style.

"Was good, tripped on my jog earlier, I'm ok now thanks."

"Yes, I noticed you walking back across the road earlier, wondered why you were walking."

"Luckily, I had a helping hand from a cyclist, or I may have still been laying in a puddle," he joked. He walks into the front garden, closing the gate. Jimmey is hovering over the waste height fence.

"A cyclist you say?" he asked.

"Yes, big, tall fella, Pat."

"I didn't see anyone with you; you were alone for sure." A trait of late ran up and down his spine, a cool shivery tingle.

"You saw me on my own, but there was a tall man, with a black helmet on and matching cyclists' suit," he said, confused.

"Bruce, you know me, I don't miss a thing around here, strange though."

"Yes, I don't know, I thumped my head, I must have imagined him. I need to go now, got a meeting in town soon."

"A meeting?" asks Jimmey, in his usual looking for more information tone of voice.

"Yes, got to go now, I'm good, don't mean to sound rude but I need to freshen up ok." He realises he said the word 'ok' upon the click of the front door closing, cutting Jimmey off. He had no time for him and had to get his head in order. It wasn't long until he meets up with Archie. The kettle boils again, and he makes a heavily loaded cup of coffee. Sitting at the table again, he thinks about the morning. The drama, all from a jog, done so many times. He is utterly confused. Meeting Nuts in the afterlife, and being escorted back by a ghost? These events are not normal. He starts to question his sanity, wondering if it was time to light one up. There is one cigarette left on the messy drawer. He slurps on the coffee, staring over at the drawer.

His mobile bleeps on the table.

It's a message from Barclays:

***YOU HAVE BEEN PAID £125.156.00***
***ACCOUNT ENDING 70191118.***

He sits back in the chair and without any more hesitation, like a man possessed, dives over to the messy drawer, taking out the packet with the last cigarette. This time after lighting it, the kitchen back door is opened but he sits at the table. He takes in a deep breath, looking down at the cigarette, hand shaking as usual. 'I guess the brunch is all on me then' he thinks. The next hour or so pass quickly. His head scrape cleaned up nicely and luckily didn't need a stitch. He was used to patching himself up on operations. Today, he would be going for lunch sporting a large square plaster. The day progressed and the time came for him to leave for his meeting at Visocchi's. He was relieved to escape the house without Mr nosey prying around. It was just as well, because the bump on his head was sore.

The trip to Broughty went reasonably well, apart from the usual Saturday morning traffic backed up on the Tay Road Bridge. This monolith of engineering was completed in 1966, and at the time bragged a badge of being one of the longest of its kind in Europe. That is because the bridge is 1.4 miles long and is still to this day, one of the longest. The bridge ended a ferry service connecting Newport-On-Tay to Dundee; a long serving mode of transport featuring in such towns named after the service. Broughty Ferry was a prime example. This service ran for not just decades, but centuries. As long-ago as Roman times, large boats were drawn across the waters by way of a rope mechanism. Later, cables and chains were commonly used, powered by steam. He parked up in Broughty, finding a nice space for a change and away from the recently introduced 'zone' parking areas. The restaurant was about a five-minute walk from Brown Street to Gray Street.

Gray Street was of course well known for its weekly market and a certain gardener from Dunella, Maureen had a stall there. The high Street was a bustle that morning. Bruce took his time wandering down the street; he still had thirty or so minutes to go before meeting Archie. It seemed a little more interesting for him today. He was going to get to know the place much better as soon as his home was at the hotel. Today, with a fat bank balance, he thought it would be nice to look inside a shoe shop window. He turned into Brook Street and crossed over to Mostyn's, a well-known shoe shop. They had been in the town for years and Bruce had often stopped there, staring into the shop window. He never bought anything due to the prices. Today was different. In he goes, setting off an antique bell on the door.

"Good afternoon, how may I help?" He was greeted by a young woman, probably a Saturday jobber, unusually tall, longish brown, untidy hair, covered in spots. She looked like she knew nothing at all about men's footwear. He tried not to focus on her ridiculous looking silver nose-ring.

"Hi, I was just looking really, I see you have a set in the window, mid tan, laced," he said.

"Oh, yes, new in these ones, actually they are on special offer today," she said. "The Oxfords, great shoes, would you like to see them?"

"Yes please, I don't have too long, but yes, I'd like that," he said. She grabbed a key from a box next to the till and made her way over to the drawer units opposite. The unit reached from floor to ceiling and was made up entirely of separate drawers.

"What's your size?"

"I'm a size ten on a good day."

She fiddles with a lock and starts to turn the key.

"Are you local?" she asks.

"No, I'm from Leuchars camp, but I will be local soon," he replied.

"I see, moving here are we, for work or something else?" She placed a pair of shoes onto a table between two chairs.

"Yes, more of a business venture," he replies.

"Take a seat, try them on and let me know what you think." He pulls off his weathered old Clarkes and slips on a new shoe. His foot melts into it. He stood up and felt his toes, satisfied that the shoe was a good fit. He slips into the other one. The shop keeper went off into the back of the shop for a few moments, suddenly reappearing with a small box. "There, I knew I'd put it somewhere, our new calculator." She opened up the box and walked over to him.

"What do you think?" she asks.

"These are great, so comfy." He walked up and down the middle of the shop, stopping at a long mirror to view them.

"Their Italian, best leather makers in the world," she added.

"What sort of business... are you not a soldier then?" asks the girl.

"I am, but not for long, I have acquired a hotel not far from here." She punches in a few buttons on the calculator.

"Today, these are reduced by 25%, so if you want them, it would be £165," she announces, but didn't expect the response coming.

"Holy shit!" She looks startled and says nothing."

"I'll have them." The sale was closed, and he had just said yes to the most expensive pair of shoed he'd ever bought.

"Do you want to keep them on?" she asked.

"Please, and can you throw these out?"

"Sure, pop to the till please." She places the old pair into a bag by the till and tings through the cost. Bruce took out his cash card and placed it on the reader. After a few beeps, he was £165 the lighter, but there was plenty more where that came from.

"What hotel have you got?" she asks as she hands over the receipt.

"The Dunella." She pulls a smirk and twitches her nose.

"Oh, really, the haunted hotel!"

"Haunted, is it?" he asks.

"Mr, everyone in the town knows about that place, it's got a few stories to tell, that's all I'm going to say. Your plaster on your head, it's flapping off," she said, offering him a tissue. He felt his plaster and indeed it was flapping, revealing the small gash. He had started to sweat in the shop and that was probably brought on with the amount of money he had just spent. She disappeared into the back shop again.

"Here, pick the right one," she said, handing him a box of Elastoplast. He selected the right size and placed it over the wound.

"That's better, suits you, soldier," said the girl.

He checked the time; it was almost 12pm. With a few minutes to spare he would make it bang on time. He thanked the girl and headed off up to Visocci's. He didn't think too much about her 'haunted' comment as he enjoyed the feeling of expensive Italian leather wrapped around his feet. He arrived at Visocchi's, typically bang on the dot. The restaurant used to be a cheap cafe, attracting workman for breakfasts until it was taken over by an Italian family in the early noughties. The place was modernised, starting to boast an expensive menu. However, that market didn't quite fit Broughty and soon they climbed down a rung or two on the ladder, returning it to a more cafe type of establishment. The posh Italian name remained though, and people still refer to it as a restaurant.

He enters, taking a look around, noting that there were a handful of people, a couple of old gents a mum with a toddler in a pram, etc. No sign of Archie. For that time of day, it seemed unusually quiet.

"Hello, table for one?" said a male voice. He turned to see a young lad, almost a male copy of the young lady in the shoe shop. Obviously, the Saturday jobbers were out in force.

"No, a table for two please, my colleague is due any minute," he replied.

"Table over here by the window, is that ok?"

"Perfect, thanks," he replied. He stares out at the passing traffic, feeling his forehead again, making sure the new plaster is on. He checks his watch. It's now a few minutes past midday. He recalled Archie was late for the meeting at the hotel. Lateness is a personal pet hate of his, especially being from a military background. The young waiter shows up and flops out a pad.

"Can I get you a drink sir?"

"Oh, yes please, a strong coffee please."

"Milk?"

"Not too much, thanks, oh and a glass of water thanks." The young waiter brings over the order, placing the cup and saucer down carefully. Bruce noted the cup was a little small and asks for a larger one.

"Can I have another please, a larger cup or mug even?"

"Of course, sir, be right over." It's now 12.20pm, still no sign of Archie. He watches people scurrying up and down the street, admiring the busy nature of the street. The busier the better for a small town, especially if you have rooms to sell in a large hotel. The chink of China and glass, fill the air as the waiter places his large fresh cup of coffee down, clattering the water bottle.

"Here we are sir; are you ordering food?"

"Yes, I'll give it until 12.30, if my colleague doesn't arrive by then, I'll be ordering for myself." The waiter starts to head off, but Bruce has a question first.

"I meant to mention this to the girl who served me in Mostyn's, about a job proposition."

"Oh, Katey, we are pals, went to school together, at college now. What's the proposition?" he asks.

"I'm employing staff up at Dunella soon and I need to get full and part-time staff if you or your friends are interested." The waiter nods and pauses for a few moments, looking around towards the counter.

"I would consider it, and I'm sure Katey would too; the wages here are shite," he whispered. He thanks Bruce and heads off to the counter. Bruce was happy that he had put it out there to the local community that things were happening at the hotel. He was banking on the seed taking root, knowing how rumour spread like a wildfire between young men and women on camp. He takes a big gulp of coffee until a knock at the window comes, causing him to nearly choke on it. It was Archie.

"Hello sir, table for one?" the waiter asks. He points over to Bruce.

"Your colleague is here sir." Archie joins him, hanging his jacket on the back of his chair. Bruce noted that today for a change he was dressed smart and wasn't in his usual workman's attire.

"Apologies, I'm late again, bloody mobile, I told you it broke," he said. Bruce hated excuses for lateness but reminded himself rapidly that here he wasn't a Staff sergeant.

"It's, ok, it happens...what happened?"

"I got on my bike and there was a ruddy puncture, on the back wheel. No time to repair it so I walked here," he said. Bruce accepted that as a reasonable excuse.

"What's a matter with your head?"

"Oh, that right there, is a long story, its fine, just a bump." Archie pulls out a small notepad from his jacket and places it in front of Bruce.

"That there, is a plan of action for the reopening of your new hotel," he says proudly. Bruce picks up the notepad and flicks through it. To him it just looked like a load of scribbles, with numbers, some crossed out. It wasn't the sort of plan he was expecting to see.

"So, this might need a bit of explanation," said Bruce.

"Aye, I know that, but it's a simple plan, and was easier than I thought." He gazes intensely at Bruce as he flicks through, trying to decipher the info within.

"I'm sorry Archie, this might mean something to you, but to me, it's just scribbles and gibberish!" Archie smiled and took it back, popping it away. They ordered lunch and sat relaxing for a while. A round of coffee came followed by another as they stewed over the plan. An hour passed by, then another as they discussed money, people, dates. The conversation between a soldier and a handyman wasn't exactly riveting. However, the pair started to stamp out a plan that they could both understand. Archie was as usual key to all of this; Bruce knew that more than anybody. The beauty of the plan was in layman's terms, that many of the staff had been laid off when Alice fell ill. The hotel wasn't doing so great, and she had thought to sell up. The illness got worse and she more or less actioned redundancies that had been in the pipeline. She was reluctant to do this, but it was necessary. It all came suddenly to the staff members and without much notice, the order came to close down. Only a few months passed after this and then she passed away.

"So, you see Gordon, I can get many of them to return, subject to pay and conditions of course," said Archie.

"That's great, and like I said, I can see the youth locally are aware of Dunella. That's great if we need to source more temps etc."

"What about the GM and a number one you mentioned?" asks Bruce. "All sorted, that will be Clare Johnston, she was a temp for the last six months before closure. I have already called her, and she is keen to return."

"So, I have less than three weeks left to work at Leuchars, then that's it. What sort of time scale are we looking at?" Archie leans back in his chair and briefly looks out at the passing people.

"Look how busty this town is, and it's not holiday season just yet. The sooner the better," he said. Bruce with military blood through and through wanted a more precise date. He pushed further.

"Well, dates for the grand opening?"

"With a bit of a spruce up, a helping hand or two for me to touch up and decorate the worse.... staff training and the like, I would say six weeks from today."

"Wow, that soon, and sales?" he asks.

"That is where you can put your faith in both Dunella the brans that she was and the marketing genius that comes with Clare." And that, was that. The two men had breathed life back into a local dormant business. The conversation had allowed Bruce to all but forget his morning ordeal and he'd not once talked about that with Archie. One thing that he had acquired as a soldier was the ability to blot out horrible experiences.

"Before we part, Bruce, I'm going for a walk around Claypotts castle tomorrow afternoon. I'd like you to come, get the cobwebs oot of your head." Bruce paused for a moment, tilting his head back, trying to remember if he'd been to that castle.

"I know of it, never been, tell me it's not full of ghosts."

"Ha ha, ghosts never, there's no such thing...is there?" replied Archie who was grinning like a Cheshire cat. They arrange to meet up at 3pm. He had nothing to lose. The more he got to know Archie, the better. After all, what could possibly go wrong wandering around an old Scottish landmark.

# Chapter eight

He returned home, happy about how the meeting had gone. So much had been talked about and achieved in such a short period of time. He felt relieved that Archie had got in touch with recent employees and had a good idea about the costs involved with running Dunella. For the time being, he would preside at the house he was so used to. However, it was time to transition and get things moving.

He also knew that Archie was right about taking stock and finding time to chill out. That was why he was looking forward to a trip around Claypotts castle. At a time in his life where he had suddenly been exposed to certain strange situations, arguably paranormal, he was about to go to one of the local sites that was known to be haunted. Or at least, reported to be.

The castle, built in the 16$^{th}$ century by a wealthy landowner, was used as a private dwelling most of the time. Not many castles of the era can boast that they are still in a habitable condition, after 500 years. With such a long history, there is an inevitable history of birth, love, death and murder. There have been many sightings both in and around the castle. The most infamous spectre is that of the White Lady, but there are also sightings of the Green Lady. There is not a great deal of information available about the residents. Indeed, for a time the castle was used as a prison, incarcerating government troops after The Battle of Killiecrankie. Bruce had heard rumour of such sightings before, but he was convinced that all ancient buildings are awash with such stories. That's why he wasn't really phased by such rumour surrounding Dunella. He was more in line with the notion that other Scottish legends, namely that of the Lochness monster, were simply attributed to people over doing it on Whiskey.

Although he had started to see and feel strange things at the hotel, it would take a whole lot more for him to become a 'believer.' The castle is located in West Ferry, so not too far for him to get to in the morning.

That night, he went to bed unusually tired. He knew that he was going through an incredibly stressful time of his life. On the one hand he was over the moon with the inheritance. On the other, he was terrified. He had no immediate family to confide in and was placing all of his eggs in one basket. He was so used to being in control in his army role, but now he was being guided by a handyman that held all the cards. This was adding to the stress. He knew that he would have to transition into a new man. Only time would tell if that man can prosper running Dunella or fold, having gotten himself into a situation almost imposed upon him. He soon fell into a deep sleep.

'Mum, is that you?'

'Yes son, it's me. You forgotten me already?'

'No, I... Is this a dream?'

'Might be, probably.'

'Might be?'

He sees his mother, floating by a stream, in a beautiful setting. There are birds singing and the water flowing is a pale blue, reflecting in the sun. She had been gone for years and died suddenly, after plunging into the freezing river Brig 'O' Dee. Bruce was on tour when he got the news just before Christmas 97. Alcohol was her best friend at that time, drowning her sorrows, never accepting the death of his father, Alec. He took his own life after struggling with his injuries sustained on tour.

'Where's dad?'

'He is trapped, but I miss him so much son.'

'Trapped...where?'

'Auntie Alice, she got me involved in stuff, I shouldn't have. I tried to contact your dad, after he was gone. She is to blame, not me!'

'What? How do you mean mum?'

'He came through and things went wrong.'

'Came through, who and where?'

'You need to release him, Bruce, your dad... his soul is trapped at Dunella.' The image of his mother starts to fade away, the still waters disappear and then, Sheila is gone!

"What the, fuck my life.... woah, what?" he wakes in a sweaty panic. He sits on the edge of the bed, realising he had just suffered an awful dream. That was enough to cause him to wake, something far from normal for a man that has witnessed the horrors of war. This was different. That experience was more like a message from beyond the grave. He wipes his sweaty forehead, noticing that yet again, his plaster was missing. He got up and went to the bathroom, tugging on the pull cord. He turns on the cold-water tap, splashing his face with cold water. He checks out his face and wound in the reflection. It seems to be ok, no blood and not open like it was. That was just as well because he was having trouble keeping plasters on.

He walks back and sits on the end of the bed. He can feel the sheets damp from sweat, soaking into his boxers. He placed his head in his hands and started to think about the dream. 'What was that all about?' he thinks. He noticed how his mother looked much younger in the dream. The message was very plain. She said that his father's soul was in Dunella....but how? He laid back in bed, kicking the damp bit of sheet off the bed. He could see that it was 3.15am. The alarm religiously goes off at 5.30am so he changed it for 6.30am

Morning came and all was well. He managed to get to sleep and thankfully the rest of the night passed without issue. He went through the same morning routine, coffee, porridge and thought about a cigarette. He had smoked the last one but seeing his hand start to shake holding his mug of coffee, reminded him that it might be time to buy some more. There was one thing for sure he wasn't going to be doing. No jogging! This morning, while sitting at the kitchen table, he stewed over the past few days events. The hotel was great. He loved being there, even if at times it was a bit creepy. He liked walking around Broughty, getting to know people and doing a bit of advertising about the reopening. He was happy that the army was almost a chapter in his past. He was enjoying his newfound companionship with Archie.

All these thoughts were reinforcing the fact that all along, this had been an incredible journey, and it was far from over. For the rest of the day, he started to sort out his things. It was high time that he sorted out his wardrobe. He pulled out a bed drawer and tipped out the contents on the bedroom floor. The usual things fell out, oversized pyjamas, a couple of pillowcases, still in the cardboard packet. Three olive green military tee-shirts, all too small. An assortment of uneaten military rations and two photo albums, a red and a blue one. He knelt down amongst the items, taking hold of the blue album. As he flicked through it, he came across the usual snaps, taken on a holiday to Cyprus. He went with three mates after his first deployment to Afghanistan. That was back in 2003, not long after the US and the UK declared the Taleban a terrorist organisation, courtesy of a certain Mr Laden. The initial deployments were the worst.

He, like so many soldiers had seen the horror of war in Europe during the 90's. Bruce himself, had stumbled across a mass grave on the outskirts of Sarajevo during the war between Serbia and Croatia. While out on patrol, one of his missions was to investigate unusual earth signs, photographed by spy satellites. The grim discoveries were made and men like Bruce were involved with the task of clearing the grave sites. The army sent most squaddies to a camp in Cyprus to decompress and vent before returning to the UK. Usually, the lads ended up spending too much and drinking copious amounts of cheap alcohol. This set of pictures brought back both fond and grim memories.

He notices two pictures, tucked into the back sleeve. These were more interesting. He couldn't remember how they got there. One was of a younger mum with a younger Alice, laughing together, cigarette in hands, outside in a pub garden. The other was of them both. This time they didn't seem so happy, stood on a rainy day outside an old Church entrance. There was a clear as day sign on the left of the entrance:

The Bon-Accord Spiritualist Church. He stared at the photo, taking in the image and the atmosphere. It was true after all. His mother had been involved with Alice in spiritualism. He cleared everything away, sorting out the rubbish from what he wanted to keep. In no time, he had filled up four bin liners. He placed the photo in his jacket pocket.

Soon, it was time for the dash to the car and start the short journey to the western side of Broughty. Claypotts was on the edge of the town. On the way, he recalled that Jimmey hadn't bothered him for a while. That was one thing for sure he was going to miss and not in a fond way. It would be a relief to not be dodging Mr 'nose bag' of the century.

He eventually arrived at the carpark. Claypotts looked ominous, silhouetted in the distance by a mix of sun and cloud. Bruce was well aware that Archie was always late, so he decided to sit in the car for a few more minutes. It was 2.55pm, so as usual he was early. There were a few cars in the carpark that afternoon. It was Sunday, Bruce wondered if the place was open so late in the day. He sat and watched a trail of people, all ages leaving the main grounds of the castle. As yet, he couldn't see anyone close that resembled Archie. It was now 3.10pm, so technically, yet again, he was late. He decides to leave the car, paying for two hours only. In the distance he can hear the haunting tunes of the bagpiper, adding to the magical atmosphere. The sign did say that the castle grounds were open; and that day there was an extension on the admissions for the interior. He had always fancied going inside; it was looking like he would be.

"BRUCE!" called a familiar voice. He turned round from a railing he was leaning against to see it was Archie. He was walking out of the main gardens of the castle. He walks over to meet him.

"You good Archie?"

"Yes, something happened earlier," he said.

"Oh! What's up?"

"I arrived earlier; I've been in already." Bruce was surprised, wondering if he was just saying that.

"Well suck my socks, if I've seen Halley's comet land!" said Bruce. They headed along the entrance pathway to the main reception. On the way through an archway, Bruce could see a large square garden, full of all manner of plants and flowers. Just beyond was the doorway to the castle. Archie carried on ahead, but Bruce stopped to look up.

'What a magnificent sight,' he thought. The entire building was built from huge almost shiny- grey stones. There were several windows, still containing glass. The roofline at the top was a Scottish Baronial style; often associated with fairytale imagery. In all, a beauty, he was struggling to understand why it's associated with a ghost or two. He caught up with Archie who was already inside. There is no fee to enter Claypotts, these days that seems a bit unusual. Stood in the main lobby was an elderly man, dressed in a kilt, holding a set of bagpipes. He was dressed in a style associated with the Bonnie Prince Charlie period, circa 1740s. There was a hat on the floor full of change and the odd banknote. Archie headed through to another room, but Bruce decided to stay a bit longer while the piper started up again. Bruce recognised the tune, it was 'Scotland the Brave.' He was so used to that tune, usually played on remembrance Sunday. He stood there musing at the piper as he squeezed the bag in and out, blowing huge lungsful of air through the mouthpiece. Bruce had heard this so many times. The Scottish regiments always have pipers kicking around camp and the Royal Dragoon Guards were no acception. He rummaged around a pocket for a few coins, noting he had three-pound coins, choosing to throw in two.

"You coming in?" asks Archie, popping his head around a huge stoney door frame. Bruce pulls himself away from the haunting tunes.

"Yes, can't wait, I was just reminiscing," They are now in one of the main rooms. These were used as reception rooms back in the past. Guests would come in after tying up a horse and use the rooms as a place to throw off their filthy boots and warm up. In Scotland, the weather is about as changeable as you can get. The summers can be warm, with temperatures high enough to create perfect conditions for the dreaded midges. The winters, now that's another story. The temperatures in the Highlands can fluctuate in a typical November from five degrees above freezing to minus twenty within a matter of hours. Many a hiker and climber or even just adventurous travellers have fallen victim to the weather patterns. The answer to this over the centuries, has been the increase in the wool trade. If it wasn't for the woolly jumpers, and indeed the rise of the woollen kilt, people in the past would have been a whole lot colder.

One of the largest additions and most important feature in such buildings, courtesy of the weather, was top introduce huge fireplaces.

"Wow, look at that, what a fire range! said Bruce.

"Aye, imagine resting in front of that beast on a freezing night," said Archie. There were flames in the fire, although it was just a small section of the fire. It reached across one side of the room about three metres, huge by most standards. The mantel piece itself was impressive. That was one huge stone, spanning the whole length of the fire, and was about two feet deep. The public couldn't sit too close to the open fire. There was a red rope, attached either side, hanging off brass poles.

"There now, that's what I call a hot fire," said Archie.

"Yes, maybe we need to make sure the fires working properly at Dunella; I'm sure it's fine," replied Bruce.

"I can tell you that the fire and chimney are working perfectly fine, I'm a man of many talents Bruce," boasted Archie. They moved through the reception room on to a huge entrance way. This had a pair of double doors either side, reaching from floor to about ten feet in height. They were immense timber doors, still showing off original handles, hinges and metal studs. In fact, there was a notice board nearby explaining that they were made as replacements to the originals in 1625. That made them just shy of 400 years old.

"I'd hate to have to shoot them in," said Archie.

"What do you mean by 'shoot?' Bruce was thinking about guns at that point.

"Shoot, that's a carpenter's term for planing the door edges. You know? So that they meet nicely without letting drafts through," he explained. After admiring the grand pictures on the walls, portraits of previous owners, they headed along a wide corridor to an opening. It was candle-lit, the flickering causing an amazing ethereal reflection inside the entrance, reflecting onto the hallway slabs. It was a spiral staircase. Archie headed in first. As he started to ascend, Bruce followed close as he could. From this point, the bagpipe tunes were much quieter, but still there, causing a range of strange echoes, resonating up and down the stairwell.

"that's quite the sound hey Archie?"

"Aye, it's as if we are back in the past; wonderful," he replies.

"Where does this lead to then?" asks Bruce. Archie didn't immediately reply, catching his breath as he climbed further.

"I'm skipping the bedroom areas; heading up to the roof." Suddenly, Archie stops and makes apologies, moving into the outer wall. Three people clamber past, downward, as quick as they can. One of them, a young man in his teens doesn't look very happy. The older couple, probably his parents stay quiet, and then: "It was nothing Daniel, you're imagining things son," said the woman. They head down further, but the two of them could hear the answer as they readjust to carry on upwards.

"I'm not making it up; she was there and then she wasn't.... ok I want out of here...NOW!" the boy said, demanding his rapid exit.

"What was that about Archie?" No reply.

"ARCHIE!" he calls out. No reply again. Bruce speeds up to find that his companion was gasping for breath outside on a roof terrace.

"You ok mate?" asks Bruce.

"No..,not exactly, that almost done me in!" he replied, finally calming down, his breaths stabilising.

"That lad was heading down fast; did you hear what he was saying?" asked Bruce. Archie stands up straight and stares out over the battlements. Bruce went over to the other side, staring through a traditional squared off battlement.

"Aye, I heard, can tell he was getting away from something. Maybe he saw the Green Lady?" They both take in the view. From there they can see a commanding view of the town. That was exactly why such castles were built. Soldiers and watchmen would guard the rooftops, looking out for miles for approaching threats. Claypotts could see beyond the town, as far as another famous castle in the ferry, aptly named 'Broughty castle.' She was built just a few years before Claypotts. When the English navy threatened an attack on the shore, landing an early version of marines, The two castles would warn each other, by lighting huge fire beacons. Such beacons are still seen around our coasts to this day. It is said that as long ago as the Elizabethan era, the 1st not the 2nd, the whole of the country could light the beacons warning the entire country of imminent danger, within a matter of a couple of hours. That's very impressive considering there were no radios, or telephones.

"Imagine defending this aye, Bruce?"

"I can't, what those people had to do back then."

"Aye, imagine what it was like under siege?" They talked a while longer, exchanging such scenarios. Between the two men, it was apparent that they were getting along just fine. Bruce was really happy that he'd been asked to come along. Archie was so right about him shedding the cobwebs. Peering down, they could see more people leaving. It was 4pm now. The castle was staying open until 6pm that day, due to a certain event that was going on in the great hall. They had climbed their way past that earlier.

It had been a mixed bag of weather that afternoon, but now, the sun had gone in behind clouds and the wind got up. The temperature had started to drop significantly and standing on top of a castle some four or five storeys in height, wasn't the warmest place. However, the wind increased a lot more, out of nowhere, causing both men to step back from the battlements. The wind was creating whistles all over the place, ebbing and flowing through ancient cracks and crevices. The roof door slams shut!

"WHAT THE BOLLOCKS!" cried Bruce, He looks over at the door. It had been secured to the wall via a chain. Archie walks over to investigate. He pulls on the ancient door handle.

"It.....It's stuck." Bruce pushes in.

"Here, let me try!" He grasps the handle, struggling to even move it, let alone open the heavy door. The wind seemed to be battering onto it, causing its closure. Without warning, freezing rain batters into them. The light decreases creating a gloomy atmosphere. Suddenly as if things couldn't get any stranger! A scream from behind them, high up on a section of roof. An ear-piercing shrill scream! Both men stop fiddling with the door handle and place hands over ears. The sound was so intense that Archie dropped to his knees. Bruce dared to look around, his heart pounding as usual, terror filling his every morsel.

He dares to stare up at the source of the sound. Rain beating off his face, streaming from his head into his eyes. He rubs his eyes hard, trying to focus. The scream dissipates, allowing them to lower their hands. Archie turns and looks up at the roof area. Bruce focuses on something, something unworldly. He rubs his eyes, rain still splattering off his face. Archie panics.

"Noooo! it can't be, oh shite!" he says. Bruce can now see clearer, his brain struggling to make sense of it. He can see a murky, green mist moving from left to right. It stops, appearing to look downward at them. He can hear Archie yanking on the door in pure unadulterated panic. The vision is causing Bruce to freeze to the spot. It darts back and forth, stopping again, seeming to peer down. Then, the misty green light, takes on a form. Bruce is absolutely frozen stiff, fused to the spot. The form is feminine, a slender female body, faceless, little detail, the stones behind the image were in full view, due to the see-through nature of the apparition. The form was not masculine. THUD! THUD! THUD! Archie's banging like a madman on the door.

Bruce is so in shock; he can't turn around to offer a hand. The thumping stops. Then, silently as if it never happened, the green light fades away into nothingness. And then simultaneously, the wind dies away, and the rain is gone. Bruce is shivering uncontrollably. He looks around at Archie.

"ARCHIE!" he calls. The door is wide open and nobody is there!

"ARCHIE!" he calls out into the darkness of the open stairwell.

No reply. He doesn't hesitate, diving into the doorway. His entire being is terrified, a feeling not known in such a way. The image had brought on a terror not yet experienced in his life. Pure adrenaline was kicking in, flowing through his veins as he clambered down the stoney, winding stairwell.

"ARCHIE WHERE THE FUCK ARE YOU?" he cries out, each step as frightening as the last. The candlelight flickering adding to the devilish situation. The eerie bagpipe tune wasn't helping as it echoed and vibrated up and down the stairwell. Eventually, he passes by the great hall entrance, he recalled it being just a bit further to go.

The bagpipe music stops. Just a few more steps and he bursts into the corridor at the bottom, running like a man possessed, past the reception room and out into the entrance lobby. And there, he sees a familiar face. Archie is sat in a chair, hands over his head. He was being comforted by the piper. Bruce looked behind him, not wanting to be there a millisecond longer. Archie didn't look too good. He lifted his head up to acknowledge Bruce. The piper tilts his head back, offering a glass of water to him. The blood had drained from his face.

"Archie, you alright... what happened?"

"You know damn well what happened, you saw it too!" The piper looked at Bruce, shaking his head. Close up, he looked to be in his late sixties, a man of experience perhaps with Claypotts? Archie drank more water and fell silent, shaking from the cold or from terror.

"Your friend, he had collapsed just through the entrance to the corridor. Did you not learn 'not to run' at school?" joked the piper

"He seems ok, what went on up there?" he asks. Bruce too was catching his breath, glancing back through the corridor.

"I.... couldn't say, it was,"

"The green lady, that's what it was," said Archie, butting in suddenly. The piper made sure Archie could hold the cup ok and turned to look along the gloomy corridor.

"She's been busy the past few days."

"Who has?" asks Bruce.

"You should know laddie, you tell me!" Bruce shakes his head, refusing to believe it, his brain telling him it was imagined. But then he realised immediately that Archie had seen it too.

"Not all are so blessed with seeing her," said the piper.

"Blessed, FUCKING BLESSED!" shouted Bruce.

"I don't consider that a blessing, that was utterly terrifying." The piper picked up his bagpipes, placing them over his shoulder, and strangely started to play another tune. He stopped and said:

"Oh, I can assure you, she's quite harmless." He starts playing again, the sound this time resonating through the place. Bruce manages to stand Archie up and he helps him to the main entrance door. As they pass through, he notices a poster on a notice board.

*WELCOME TO THE INVESTIGATION OF*
*CLAYPOTTS CASTLE*
*COURTESY OF: DUNDEE PARANORMAL*
*INVESTIGATION TEAM*
*(Please arrive with an open mind!)*

'Bugger to that' he thought, as they move out into the front grounds. The haunting piper tunes started to fade away as they got to the carpark. They stopped at the car and looked back at the castle, both men silent for a moment. Archie was clutching his left arm; lifting his sleeve on his jumper revealed a bruise on his forearm. They took stock of the situation, processing what they had just witnessed.

"You alright Archie?"

"Hell, I don't know, I'll be honest, that was pure terror; nobody will ever believe it!"

"I know, I'm still shaking," replied Bruce.

"You can't say we imagined that this time."

"I'm not denying I saw it, just don't know what it really was." Yet again, Bruce bore witness to something 'out of this world' and chose to somehow disregard the vision. Archie wasn't as easily convinced.

"That was undeniable, and otherworldly; you saw it and heard it too," he said. They stare back at the castle and can see torch light moving eagerly up and down the stairwell.

"Those poor buggers don't know what their getting themselves into," said Bruce.

"I've had enough for one day lad, it's time for me to head off," said Archie. He turns to walk towards a bicycle shelter, then stops and steps back towards Bruce. He stood looking at him, expressionless at first. Then, the blood seemed to leave his ageing face again.

"You're wound....it, wait on a minute," he leans in, inspecting his forehead.

"Laddie, your wound is completely gone." Bruce leaned down to look in a wing mirror. Easing a thumb across his forehead, he can see that the unhealed dark scabbed gash and surrounding bruising had disappeared.

"You want to deny that too?" asked Archie.

"Right, no....look I don't know, ok, strange things happened up there!"

Archie stepped back and turns to walk away, as he did so he said: "Not only did you see it, but you were also touched by it!" he said as he headed to the shelter. "ARCHIE!" he calls him, momentarily putting the experience behind him. Archie stopped fiddling with his bicycle lock while Bruce walked over.

"When can you meet again at Dunella?"

"I can get there any time, but you're busy still at work, so it's up to yourself," he said.

"I can be there Saturday next, I only have a couple weeks left in the army, so I need to get moving on setting up shop there," said Bruce.

"I'll call you Friday just to make sure then."

"You got yourself a new mobile finally."

"I did, should arrive tomorrow, so I'll be in touch." said Archie. He heads off on his bike, clearly keen to get away from the castle. Bruce headed off, analysing his latest weird experience. He is shaken with the sighting. He is in two moons about the experience. On the one hand it was utterly terrifying, a situation he would never want to see repeated. On the other, it was an amazing experience. To see a legendary ghoul, must be up there with one of life's top experiences. The traffic was unusually light on his journey home. The journey was done in under twenty minutes. As he pulls into his street, he can't but notice an ambulance outside his house, parked awkwardly across his drive. He comes to a stop, parking on the bend a few cars along. As he walks to the house, two paramedics burst out of

Jimmey's front door, each one at either end of a medical trolley. They are followed out by another man, elderly looking, strangely wearing a light-yellow coloured tracksuit.

At first, Bruce couldn't quite see much, as they were obscured by a few garden bushes. And then, the trolley rumbles onto the front pavement, revealing a person on the bed. Bruce could see that it was indeed Jimmey, wearing an oxygen mask and he had a drip fed into his right arm.

"Holy shit! what's going on?" he asks the paramedics. There was silence from Jimmey. They clamber around with the rear ambulance doors, eagerly trying to get him safely on board.

"Hello, you are?" asks a female paramedic.

"I'm Bruce, his next-door neighbour; is he ok?"

"We suspect he has suffered a heart attack; he only just managed to call 999," she said. Bruce peered into the ambulance, trying to see him, but it was evident that they were giving CPR. The sound he was all too familiar with. Then, just before the doors closed, he heard the thump of an electrically charged shock. He heard it a second time, followed by a constant signal. That usually indicates a flat line. The elderly man was stood at front gate, waiting, and noticed Bruce

"Hello, are you Bruce the neighbour?" he asks.

"I am he, not seen you before; what's happened?"

"Jimmey, he's not been too well, called me last night to announce he was feeling ill. Never thought he'd have a heart attack though." he said.

"I thought he was a bit quiet earlier, he has a habit of making himself known!" said Bruce.

"Sorry, you are?" he asks the man.

"I'm Peter....Pete Duncan, a friend from his metal detecting group. He called me again today, he started to feel worse, so I told him to call 999 if he got any worse."

"Looks like he just about managed to do that, luckily," replied Bruce. They stood at the garden gate; they could hear the melee of medical paraphernalia being used on the ambulance. The paramedics had obviously decided to try to revive him urgently, before heading off to the local hospital. The feeling was tense, Bruce didn't know Pete at all and making small talk with the bleeping thrum close-by wasn't easy.

Bruce made excuses to go inside for a moment to use his downstairs toilet. While he's stood there taking a pee, he couldn't decide whether to laugh or cry. 'What a day' he thought. He pops back out and sees Pete stood talking to a medic. He waits briefly at the door, watching as the medic put an arm around Pete. He walks to the front gate.

"All ok with him?" he asks. Pete doesn't reply, but the medic has something to say: "Look, its bad news, we couldn't bring him back and we need to get to the hospital asap," he explained.

"You mean he's died?"

"Look, we can't officially confirm that until a doctor inspects him at casualty; I can't say too much at the moment." Bruce knew from experience that they were being a bit sheepish about giving too much away. Its common practice for a doctor to officially confirm a death. Ridiculous as it sounds, even in a battle situation when a buddy is split into four pieces and clearly dead, it's not official until a doctors say so. The ambulance starts up, lights blazing away. Pete asks Bruce to close the front door to Jimmey's house while he takes a ride to the hospital with the medics. He watches as they drive off, full bells and whistles blaring.

He heads to the front door, realising that in so many years of knowing Jimmey, he had only been in the house once. They were far from close. It's often the case that a neighbour, especially one directly next door, can be so distant. From inside, he hears the telephone ring. He is looking for the simplest way to lock the front door, but the telephone doesn't stop. He made the decision to answer it, as it was probably someone who had wind of Jimmey's bad news. He rushes through into the kitchen and answers the call.

"Erm, hi, how can I help?" he asks. A panicky female voice replies.

"Oh, hello, what's going on, what's happened, who.... where is Jimmey?" she cries.

"I'm his neighbour, he's been taken ill and is off to hospital."

"Oh my, hospital...Pete called me to let me know he was in a bad way, and the line got cut off," she said.

"Yes, I expect he called you just before or straight after getting here. May I ask how you know Jimmey?" The caller calms down a little, but she's clearly shaken up. She explains that she was a daughter, calling from Devon. Bruce had never met her or even knew that he had a daughter. He had mentioned children by his long since divorced wife but never talked about them with Bruce. Likewise, Jimmey didn't know much about his family either. He left the caller with the hospital details before turning off all the lights and closing the inner front door and porch. The events of the day were starting to play on his mind. It didn't look too good for Jimmey, but Pete agreed to call him as soon as he knew more, having took his number at the garden gate.

He jumps in the shower, washing the day away, as best he could. Before heading to bed, he has one last mission of the day, making a double heaped spoon of coffee, with a double dose of sugar. He sits at the table yet again, questioning the days experiences. And then, his mobile rings.

"Hi, Bruce, its Pete."

"Hi Pete, any news?"

"Yes, look I won't keep you, but I think we both knew he was gone."

"Shit, is he dead?"

"Yes, he's no longer with us!"

"Ok, look thanks for letting me know; I spoke to his daughter earlier."

"Ah yes, Denise, she's taking it badly, I have updated her too."

"Right, well the house is secure, let her know if I can help in any way, I'm here ok." The call ends, he downs the rest of his coffee, shaking his head in disbelief. Eventually, he makes it up to bed, it's later than usual and work is in the morning. He leaves the bedside table lamp on, staring up at the ceiling. With so much spinning around his head, it was going to be another strange night. For the first time, in a long time, he felt alone. That was a strange thought, and it was entirely due to the fact he knew his annoying neighbour had died, that day. Bruce was an end terrace and on the other side of his house was just a pathway that school kids and dog walkers used to cut through from an estate close by. That led to the main track, or pathway that he was so used to running along.

It was only the other day that Jimmey had seen him crossing over the road, without the cyclist 'Pat' who helped him home. He started to rethink so much, trying his best to rationalise everything. It was undeniable that he had seen the image of a green woman that afternoon. It was undeniable that he had a strange 'otherworldly' encounter when he hit his head out jogging. It was undeniable also that his recently departed neighbour had seen him without his ghostly companion that morning.

The creepy image of a shadow figure up at Dunellas' window, the sounds he heard there. To top it all off, the creepy dream of his dearly departed mother! Was it a dream or was it a message from beyond the grave? He starts to doze off, briefly awaking, then heading off again. The pattern continues, he tosses and turns, staring back at the ceiling. Then, as if things couldn't get any worse.

"THUD! THUD! THUD! He wakes from a light sleep, not moving a muscle, peering over at the wall clock. It was midnight. 'Am I dreaming?' he thinks.

"THUD! THUD! THUD! Louder this time. He sits up in bed, and swings his legs around, placing his feet on the floor. He dared not move, waiting for the sound to repeat. He had no idea where it was coming from. He gets up and looks out of the window. He can see down to the front door, but there's nobody there. He stands at the window for a few more moments. Once more, the noise repeats, this time, he knew for certain it was coming from next door. The noise of thuds were coming from the adjoining front bedroom wall. He freezes.

"This can't be happening!" he says out loud. He stares out of the window again, checking Jimmey's front door. Its closed. He sits back on the bed, staring at the wall.... Suddenly: BLEEP! BLEEP! BLEEP! The alarm sounds, causing him to jump up in bed, wiping his face. He is totally bemused. The second time in almost as many nights that he had suffered a nightmare. He sat up, staring at the wall. He swore that just moments ago, it was midnight, and he was trying to work out an unknown noise from next door.

The morning daylight, bathes his bedroom in a welcome sunny light, easing his unsettled mind. Yet again, another bad dream. Another realistic dream. 'Was that bloody Jimmey?' he thinks, instantly rubbishing the thought. He rules out that the banging was coming from a paranormal source. It was just way too creepy to even go there, especially as Jimmey had just passed away. He thinks about the experience at Claypotts. He gets ready for work, dismissing the night. The next few evenings would be taken up sorting belongings out, ready for moving as much as he could by the weekend.

Friday eventually comes; the previous few nights had passed by relatively peaceful. However, the dreams persisted, a combination of his mother and the Claypotts experience causing him to wake up almost each night. The strange 'THUD' noises didn't repeat, so he dismissed that as a passing idiot playing a prank; although he knew deep down, it was something else. He had managed to sift through plenty of his belongings, boxing stuff up ready to take to the hotel on Saturday. He spoke to Chloe again, about her possible involvement with the hotel soon. Things were looking very positive. She happened to know a friend that was starting out as a 'man and van' business, recommending him to help with his eventual move. He arranges for the move to take place in a couple of weeks. That meant that he had only two weeks left in the house.

It was Saturday morning. The sun was out; he had been awake since 5.30am. Over the past few days, he had bought a stack of cardboard, ready to assemble into moving boxes. He had started to label them up. Lounge bits; kitchen; bathroom; shed stuff, blah blah. He was surprised to see around thirty boxes, large, medium and small scattered around the kitchen, living room and stacked out in the hall. The house was looking bare. His car was packed full of boxes, rubbish and old rugs, mixed up with a couple of old lampshades and unwanted boots. He wasn't a fan of his car of several years, a faded red Peugeot 406, having few bells and whistles, but it was an estate, so finally he appreciated its size. He had a chat with Archie the night before as planned. He was still rattled with what they had seen at the castle. He soon settled down on the subject when Bruce explained that on the same day, 'Mr nosey' had died suddenly. Bruce decided not to tell him about the bangs from next door and his strange dreams. In fact, he was just trying to put aside all the shenanigans of recent days, concentrating more on his preparation to move.

 He left the house as per usual, but this time it was a bit different. He still peered around the porch corner, trying to spot Jimmey. He was sad now, feeling a bit of shame about how he used to treat him. There had been a few strangers in and out of his house, blocking his route in and out of his drive, but he assumed they were friends or family, sorting out his affairs. With that in mind, he parked further down on the corner, not bothering them at this sad time. Today was going to be a busy one again. First the dump, now of course known as Balvodie recycling centre, just outside Broughty Ferry; the formal name and old practices had changed just a week before. He didn't know it yet, but the old dump with the waste height concrete wall had gone. Now, instead of backing up to it, throwing everything and your dog over the wall, you have to choose metal container sections. The process would take three times longer than usual.

 The deed was done, and luckily as it was still quite early, before 9am, he was one of only three or four using the dump. It was different, clambering up and down the damp steps and railings, to the huge metal containers, but sometimes change is done in an effort to reverse the damage done from decades of non-recycling. This was all just another part of life changes that he was apparently not always in control of. He headed out of Balvodie and drove a few minutes more to Dunella.

# Chapter nine

He pulled into Dunella's drive, admiring the majesty of the building bathed in morning sunlight. It all looked so different and less foreboding in the sun. It was mid-June now and the gardens were looking fresh, full of flowers and shrubs. The grassy area within the circular drive was looking quite long. He guessed it would have been a whole lot worse, if it wasn't for Archie keeping on top of things during the winter months.

He parked in the usual spot, only this time there was another car close by. He had never seen it before, another Peugeot, but a small green 206. He wound the window down, staring across to the main entrance. There didn't look like anyone was there yet and Archie would never arrive before him. Having said that, he did show up before him at Claypotts castle. Although he had his own entrance keys now, he wanted to wait for Archie, knowing that it was less likely he'd mess up the alarm sequence. Suddenly, appearing from the rosebush archway from the rear grounds, he saw a woman. She didn't notice him at first as she passed the cars and made her way towards the entrance to

reception. She was average height, with light brown hair tied in a bun. She had blue jeans on that didn't exactly help her as Bruce thought she was a bit podgy. For a nice warm day, her choice of clothing was a ridiculous looking green sleeveless shirt, so tight that her large breasts were just huge. He honked the horn, causing the woman to turn at look immediately. She smiled over at him and headed towards the car. He got out to meet her.

"Hi, I'm Bruce, can I help you?"

"Oh, Bruce, I've heard so much about you," she replied. "I'm Clare," she said. They shook hands and stood for a moment; she notices something on his forehead.

"Oh, your head, its bleeding," she said. He feels his head, wondering why as far as he knew it was miraculously healed at Claypotts.

"Blast it, I thought that had gone!" he said, feeling it again and wiping a few drops of blood on his trousers.

"Gone? That's not going anywhere fast; a wound that size." She rummages around her small handbag and pulls out a small packet of tissues. He takes one and heads back over to his car, pulling the wing mirror out to inspect the wound. He dabs the blood and thinks: 'Bloody weird that, it was gone, now its back...why?'

She walks over to him, and satisfied its stopped bleeding, he pushes the wing mirror back in place.

"Archie did mention you, that you worked here once?" he asks her.

"Yes, I did, I was a GM for a while, just before the owner sadly passed. I was laid off, well fired if you like, as were the others."

"That's too bad, you were the manager, that's some role in a place this size," he said.

"I loved it here, I was a temp, through 'Key Personnel Dundee.' I started here as a sort of P.A to Mrs Dogherty, I did get to call her Alice though," she said.

"My Aunt Alice, that would be, I didn't see her much, but what a wonderful place she had," he said.

"Yes, absolutely, and it's all yours now," she added.

"I know, I love it and all her stories that came with her." Clare took out a pack of cigarettes, lighting one up, just after she offered him one, of which he refused. Bruce went back to the car and opened the boot, readying the offload he had ahead of him.

"Oh Bruce, I could tell you a thing or two about this place," she said. He starts to lift boxes out and he can here Clare talking to someone. Its Archie. Bruce notes its only 9.20am by that point, just twenty minutes later than planned. He carries on offloading while Archie took Clare inside, silencing the inevitable bleep bleep from the alarm. A short while later, Archie appeared from the far side of the building. He was pulling a four-wheeled trolley. Bruce finished off emptying his boot, just as he caught sight of him.

"Here you go Bruce, this will come in handy. Do you need a hand?"

"No, I'm all good, you get on and sort out Clare."

"Ok, that's fine, I've left the side fire escape open for you. It leads to the corridor with the lift in," he said.

"Great and thanks Archie." He starts to head off, but Bruce calls him back for a moment and asks:

"You alright after what happened at the weekend?" He walks back to him, and side swipes a foot across the gravel, staring down, looking a bit down in the dumps. "You know, we did see her, didn't we?"

"I assume you mean the green lady?" replies Bruce.

"Who else would I mean?"

"I can't say for certain, but honestly, the image of a woman taking form, after the blood curdling scream, along with the green see-through mist. It must have been her." He starts to lift a box or two onto the trolley.

"It might help you to feel a bit more relaxed around here," said Archie.

"And what does that mean?"

"If you are accepting that such experiences are paranormal, it may help you, that's all I'm saying," said Archie. Bruce didn't reply, choosing to load up the trolley while Archie went back inside.

He starts to think how nice it is listening to children playing in the rear grounds. It sounds like a couple of girls and maybe a boy. He assumes that Clare had brought them and carries on loading up. He closes the boot and heads off pulling the trolley to the side fire escape. This will be one of two trips he guestimates, not worrying about the boxes by his car.

"Hey Mr!" He hears a child's voice, stops and looks around. He can't see anyone, only his car and the rest of his stuff. He carries on until: "HEY MR!" louder this time, two voices simultaneously. He stops again, looking back. He sees nothing. Ignoring it as kids' horseplay he carries on to the side entrance. He enters the corridor, pulling the trolley to the lift. He hadn't noticed the lift on the last two visits. It was nothing special, just a worn gold coloured paint on a couple of slide doors. There were a few symbols, mounted above the doors, with a hand, like those on a clock in the centre. The options were B, G, 1, 2, and that was all. He recalled that the PS or private suite, also known as the terrace, was at the top of a set of stairs. So, the assumption he made was that 'G' was actually for the cellar, then 1st 2nd after ground. Seemed straight forward enough. The only thing was, he would have to unload on the 2nd floor then work out how to carry the rest up to the PS. He finished offloading the trolley and had left himself a space for himself to get inside. He was about to press 2nd when:

"Hey, I said Mr!" To say he jumped was an understatement. He almost suffered a heart attack, because that voice of a child came from right behind him. He looked round instantly, to see nobody there.

"WHO IS IT?" he calls out. No reply. "ITS NOT FUNNY ONE BIT!" he calls out. Still nothing, just silence. He turns back about to press the button again but this time another call to him, but two or maybe three voices at the same time: "COME GET US OLD MAN!"

Enough was enough, the voices were so close, they must be just around the corner from the fire exit. He runs outside, looking to his left and right. Nothing. He carries on back around the building, looking across the drive to his car, only to be met with Clare and Archie.

"Bloody kids, did you bring them with you?" he asks, as he stops for a breath. She looks at Archie, shaking her head.

"I don't have kids Bruce, what's going on?" He carries on past them both heading towards the rear grounds, not running but walking with purpose. They turn to watch him disappear through the rose archway.

"COME OUT YOU LITTLE SHITS!" he shouts, in an angry voice. Meanwhile. "He's seen them do you think?" asks Archie.

"No, they are rarely seen. He is so tuned in, but doesn't know it yet," she said, nodding. "You were right Archie; he has his auntie's gift for sure!" He comes back a minute or so later, looking red in the face.

"I can't be done with this shit, guess that was a bloody ghost or ghosts, right?" he said angrily, stopping to look back through the archway.

"What happened?" asks Archie.

"Don't, ask, look After all the weird stuff that's gone on lately, I'm not accepting that there are ghost kids here too. Nonsense, just nonsense!" Bruce is angry, frustrated and fed up. He has been analysing events, trying to come to his own conclusion. This is all he needed. He walks back to the lift at pace.

"You have told him about this place have you not?" Clare said to Archie.

"Aye, well...bits you know, the man is moving in soon, I can't be scaring him off,"

"I see, do you think he can cope?" asks Clare.

"He's a pretty robust, type with strong strength of mind, I can't control them. You know how they respond to change, and the reawakening of the hotel is stirring something up." Clare had worked for several months at Dunella. Although she was brought in to help Alice with the running of Dunella, she was well known by her. Clare was a friend who she met at the spiritualist church. She was in her mid-thirties now, but from a young age, she could do strange things. At the age of just six, she had an imaginary friend at her home not far from the hotel. She called him 'soldier.' Her parents just accepted that 'soldier' was the invention of a young child. Children have created such beings for millennia; however, it has been accepted for a long time, within the spiritualist community that they are not always just an imaginary being. It has been accepted as the first sign that a child may have a gift. In Scotland, that gift is commonly known as 'the third eye.'

She would be seen playing in the back garden with 'soldier' often, at times she would sit talking to thin air. She could be heard talking to him at night, when she was alone in her bedroom. Her parents accepted this for many months until one freezing cold Saturday morning. Her mother came downstairs as she had done a thousand times before, expecting to see Clare sat in the lounge watching Saturday kids TV. In 1980 her favourites were Care Bear cartoons and Fraggle Rock, both of which were huge hits then. That morning, mum walked into the lounge and couldn't see her. The TV was off. She called upstairs but there was an unusual silence. Dad was still having a lay in, so she went upstairs to check her bedroom. She wasn't there.

With panic setting in, she bolted downstairs, checking all the rooms. She was nowhere to be seen. Then she noticed the kitchen door slightly open. The freezing draft whipped up around her ankles. She wasn't prepared for what she was about to find. She threw on a coat and slippers and went out to the back garden. Clare was in the garden swing, but the swing was being pushed by something unseen! Her mother stopped in shock and called her. She was murmuring a strange tune, and didn't look at her mother. She called out to her and the swing stopped. When she rushed over to Clare, she was unconscious, still and looked blue with the cold. They took her inside to warm her up and eventually she was fine, but she kept saying 'soldier' wanted to play.

That sight was never fully explained. Her mother knew what she had seen, and her father rubbished it as imagined, or even sleepwalking. This was just one of many similarly spooky events. As she grew older, in her early teens, she could tell her parents and friends stories about people that they knew or had known. This was always strange because her accounts were factual and she herself had never met them. Her family knew that she was dabbling in the dark arts. She would often lay out a cup or two, surrounded by letters and numbers. This was a makeshift Ouija board. As she grew older, 'soldier' seemed to go, but she contacted numerous souls from beyond. She got so good at it that friends and family would pop in to have readings done. She didn't like to set up formal séance sessions, but she did like to do something else.

Clare would sit with a friend of her mothers, or a family member and ask them to give her an item. It had to be something once alive, for example a leather wallet, belt or purse. She would fall into a trance and start rubbing the item. Then, within a few seconds only, she would experience pictures and visions; all of which were linked in some way to the person's family or past. Clare got so good at this, that word spread and she was locally known as 'The Witch.' She hated that and always laughed it off, but she couldn't shake off the third eye. It is something you are born with. Eventually as she grew older, she joined a couple of spiritualist clubs. Eventually, she would meet Alice.

Meanwhile, Bruce was back at the elevator, convinced the pesky kids had got into the grounds just messing around. Finally, he pushed the 2$^{nd}$ floor button and waited for the lift to do its magic. It was slow, but it worked and was especially useful for him that morning. On the 2$^{nd}$ floor, he started to offload his boxes and other belongings. It was going to take some time to get his things along the corridor to the back stairs, but he had little option, thanks to the lift stopping on the 2$^{nd}$ floor. After shuffling the boxes along the corridor and up the rear stairwell, he was eager to get into the private suite. There was a small brown envelope at the foot of the door:

## PS suite keys

'Great' he thought and went inside. It was a great place, modern and clean. The viewing he had with Archie was good, but he could now explore his new home properly. He pulled in the last of the first load and started to place the relevant boxes in the right rooms. Soon, he left his apartment and headed back down to reception, taking the lift in a bid to preserve his energy. After all, it was getting on for 11am by now and he was long overdue a strong coffee. He passed reception and heard Clare talking to Archie. The voices were coming from the office behind reception. He noted that they seemed to be arguing about procedure and things that he knew little about. So, he conveniently walked by and made his way out to the car.

Just as he reached the car, he hears another voice and turns around. He just caught sight of a young woman about to go into reception. He recognised her and called over. It was definitely her, recognisable by her long shaggy long hair, dress that wouldn't go a miss at a Marilyn Manson concert, and that nose piercing. "Hi, I said hello, but you were almost at your car," she said. It was Katey from the shoe shop.

"Well, hello, Katey, how's things?"

"Great, well not that great I suppose, I remember you said there might be an opportunity here, so here I am."

"You might have turned up on the right day at the right time. The general manager to be id inside," he said.

"Brills, oh, how did you know my name, we don't have name badges as such," she said.

"Your friend at Visocci's, he told me when I was in for Lunch."

"Well, I can tell you that Broughty never keeps a secret. Everyone knows everything about each other!" she said. Bruce grabbed a box and started to place it on the trolley. "I'm Bruce by the way, incase I never said the other day."

"Great Bruce, I'll leave you to get on; I start at 1pm today so I don't have too long here," she said and went inside. He finally got the rest of his belongings upstairs and sorted the rest of the boxes out. It was time for coffee and again headed down. This time, he took the rear stairs, and just like the other day with Archie, the creepy whistling was doing its thing. However, that didn't seem nearly so eerie on a sunny morning, compared to that of a windy dark evening.

Down at reception, it was nice to hear voices, chit chatting away, filling the normally dead atmosphere with something positive and fresh.

Clare was heading into the Culloden room, while Archie was sat by reception. "How did you get on with your stuff?" asks Archie.

"Good, I feel much better now I'm almost in," He noted that Archie was fiddling around with several telephone wires, all attached to two or three black telephones.

"I need to get reception sorted soon, or you'll not get many telephone enquiries," he said.

"Yes, true, I need something very important Archie, like right now!"

"Oh, Mr head of operations, what might that be?"

"A coffee, there seems to be bugger all here!" Archie points to the Culloden room. "In there, if your quick!"

He takes that as a good enough sign there's coffee on the go. Opening the double doors, the waft of fresh coffee hits his nostrils immediately. In the room, sat at a long table, pulled out from the side of the wall, were three ladies. He recognised Clare and Katey, but there was a third. She was a petite looking woman, sat with her back to him. Clare looks up. "Hi Bruce, you good?"

"Yes, great smell is that, where is the coffee, I'm almost collapsing here!" he said.

"Just there on the bar, would you mind bringing the tray over please?" He goes to the bar and there's a nice fresh boiled coffee jug, filled with lovely black coffee. He puts the jug on the tray, already overladen with four cups, a pot of cream and a small dish filled with white and brown sugar cubes. He takes it over to the table as asked, making the mental note that Clare was indeed the managerial type.

"There we are ladies," he said, carefully placing the contents onto the table. The strange woman looked up at him and smiled. He wasn't expecting her to look so old. From the back, first impressions were that of a woman in her twenties, but she was more like late fifties or early sixties. She had black hair and was wearing a black Nike cap. She had olive brown skin, and she smiled at him; revealing two missing front teeth.

"This is Magda," said Clare.

"Bruce offered his hand out to shake hers, but she just smiled again and ignored that.

"Hello Magda, coffee?" he asks.

You grab a seat, I'll do that Bruce," said Clare, in her authoritative manner. She proceeded to pour out three cups, Katey had said that she wanted a coke, but they were not at the bar. He sat down opposite Magda, as she stared at him with her aged face, and little grin. He put four sugars into his cup and took a swig. He immediately felt better for it. "Apologies for gate crashing the meeting ladies, I had to have a hit," he said, "A hit, you mean drugs?" asked Katey.

"Ha, not that sort of hit, at my age a hit is a strong coffee," he joked. So, what's going on?" he asks.

"We have been getting a whole lot ready this morning," said Clare.

"Oh, what sort of stuff," he asks. She went quiet for a moment, as if the question wasn't worth the answer.

"Stuff!" she said. He takes a larger swig on the coffee, not satisfied with that answer. Magda started to giggle. Bruce was a bit taken a-back by the awkwardness that was going on.

"So, Katey, have you got the job?"

"Aye, I believe so, I'm really grateful. That shoe shop isn't my scene," Clare is scribbling into a notebook, nodding slightly and says:

"Yeah, she has, and we need good people here, Dunella always demands the best."

"Hmm, right, ok, anything else I need to know?" he asks further. There's another pause, as the writing carries on. Clare stops and looks at him, slamming a hand on the table.

"Mr Gordon, Archie could do with a hand I'm sure, she said. He finishes his coffee and thanks them for it and headed back to reception. Archie isn't there. He thinks for a moment about how rude Clare came across, but then given her task, he just thought it was probably how it's going to be. 'Owning the hotel is one thing, running it is another,' he thinks to himself.

"Hey pal!" from close behind him. He turns to see Archie.

"Holy shit, please, you'll see me in an early grave!"

"Oops, sorry, I was at the telephone hub, there are a few issues," he said.

"What like?"

"The lines are dead right now, and I'm trying to fathom out why," said Archie.

"Should we not get BT in to check it out?" Archie throws a couple more wires on the reception counter.

"Not yet, I will save you money if I can, I'll sort it before Monday."

"What's going on here Monday?" he asks, sensing they were keeping something from him.

Clare is confident she can the reception up and running this Monday. That's the money shot Bruce,"

"Money shot?" he asks.

"Aye, the bookings, she's already put it out in the local paper and online about the reopening date," he said. Archie told him the plans. They were only properly made that morning. Bruce was so busy moving his things into the 'PS' that he had no idea of the progress being made. He did ask Archie about Clare's blunt attitude towards him, but he explained that it's nothing personal; just business. He also explained to him that he needs to trust in the team that was being reformed, with new additions such as Katey. The date was set for Friday June fifteenth. That was next week.

Suddenly, the Culloden door swung open, with Magda and Katey chatting away, heading out to the main entrance. Clare called them over from reception. "Guys, can you pop in here a mo?"

They go into Culloden where it appears she has made another fresh jug of coffee. They sat with her at the same long table. This time, Archie did the honours with the coffee.

"Right, we are all set for Friday 15th, the cleaner is sorted as is the head housekeeper, and reception is staffed," she announces, running her finger down the long list. It turned out Magda is not only a cleaner, but head of housekeeping too. She is introducing two others from Monday to make up the bedrooms. Katey was down to assist Clare with reception for the time being.

"Maintenance sorted, you of course Archie," she said. "That leaves you Bruce."

"Me?"

"Yes....you!" she said. He didn't quite know what to say to that, as he hadn't once thought about an actual role at the hotel.

"I could use a pair of hands to get a few bits done," said Archie.

"That's sorted then any questions?"

"Yes, just a couple, of points, I'm shit at DIY and gardening too," said Bruce. She closed her notepad and finished her last mouthful of coffee, before getting up.

"You'll be fine, won't he Archie?"

"Aye, I'll keep him busy, don't worry." Bruce was in the dark from the bulk of the plans made. With all the stress he had been experiencing lately, he felt that it was probably a good thing. After all, he knew that deep down, he knew little to zero about being a hotelier. However, one thing he hadn't banked on when he stepped into the ring (so to speak) was being made a 'caretakers' assistant. Coming from a background of ordering troops around, this wasn't going to sit well with him. He realised that on top of this, it was looking likely he would be moving in earlier than was thought. As the hotel was planned to open full bells and whistles in just a week from now, it was probably a good idea to be fully moved in by then.

It was around 2pm by now, Clare was marching up and down with Archie, making notes and checking equipment. She had been involved heavily with the close down, just after Alice fell ill, ordering the redundancies, leading to full closure. Because of that, she was familiar with everything, and it appeared that most things important to the re-opening were already in place. She had placed another important sheet of paper on the counter. Bruce decided to have a peek:

*1  Sort out kitchen equipment (Magda team)*

*2  Gas and electrical inspections)*

*3  Ensure East Dundee culinary services deliver on time*

*4  Get bedrooms ready (Magda team)*

*5  Window cleaner*

The list went on, touching on things he had never had to consider in his life. He hears footsteps so puts it back.

"Having a nosey are we Bruce?" asks Clare. She's stood there with Archie, looking up at a lamp dangling at height in reception.

"That needs a good clean too," she says to Archie, he makes another note. Bruce chose not to answer or say anything as they disappeared into the gent's toilet. He decided to go for a wander outside as it was still a nice sunny day. On doing so, he passed his car on-route to the rear grounds. He noticed something a bit unusual. His car was never the cleanest and he had washed it a month or so ago. Upon closer inspection, he could see lettering marked into the grimy bonnet:

Mr Mr Mr     Old man         old man

Mr Mr            old man     hey old man   Mr

   This was something else. He took stock of this, trying to analyse what he was seeing. The writing was in an old-fashioned style. Convinced there were kids around the rear grounds, he went to look around. The grounds were empty, only birdsong going on and a neighbour's dog barking. He walked up to the far end, until he came to one of the two ponds. Not a soul in sight, at least he thought that.
   "COME OUT I KNOW YOURE ABOUT!" he cries out, utterly convinced they were there. He hears a giggle or two.
   "ITS NOT FUNNY, COME SHOW YOURSELVES!" he shouts out. Still nothing. He stood still for a moment or two, soaking up the now late afternoon atmosphere. He looks around, taking notice of how long the grass had got since he was there the last time. He's not convinced at all. He waits between the two ponds, crouching down. Nothing is there, not a sound, not a single murmur. He looks at the pond water; it was very dirty and ponged a lot. Suddenly, without warning, a simultaneous giggle from behind, followed by a BOO! Startled, he slips forward and straight into the pond. In he went, headfirst, his lower body submerged, only his legs from the upper thighs were exposed. He clambers around the bottom, his hands slipping on the slimy concrete bottom. He holds his breath, feeling for the sides, as filthy water entered his ears and mouth, mouth and nostrils. He panics as his arms are flailing around, his upper body still submerged. Just as he starts to lose the fight to get out, a pair of hands plunge into the water, grabbing his neck and lifting his head above the surface. In the murky blurriness his eyes were experiencing, he can make out a woman, stood at the side. She offers him another hand, and he manages to clamber out, almost completely drenched through. He sat down and took a breath after coughing out a few leaves and pond debris.

"Bloody hell, I nearly drowned in that little pond," he said. The woman was stood there looking into the water.

"Thank you for helping me out." She stared at him, silent at first and then said: "I know how dangerous it can be, the pond," she said. Bruce stood up, water draining from all over. He focused on his apparent heroin, who looked about in her 60s brown hair, in a bob wearing gardening type clothing. He noticed she had a droopy left eye and on the same side of her head was a peculiar looking indentation. Not knowing her, he didn't delve into a stranger's physical peculiarities.

"And how is that he asked her?"

"Oh, I used to work here, long ago, I was the gardener," she said.

"Great, are you looking for a job?" She turned from her gaze at the water and looked directly at him.

"No, I can't work anymore, I haven't for a long time now,"

"Well look, I need to go in or I'll freeze to death, you want to pop in for anything; what's your name?" She fell silent for a few moments, strangely going quiet again, as if in a trance.

"I am Maureen, and I am still around, even though I can't work," she said. He turned to start his way back to the hotel.

"Look the least I can do is introduce you to a couple of people, the hotel is opening soon," he said.

"Yes, I'd like that, Bruce," They start walking along the overgrown path by the side of the main lawn. He can hear her close, stepping on the odd twig and dry leaves.

"Hey, Maureen, how do you know my name, have we met?" he asks, still in front, expecting a reply. With no answer, he turns around. Maureen is gone. He stops and looks around, wiping his eyes, listening. Chills are running up and down his spine. A combination of the water-soaked clothing and an experience with a woman who apparently wasn't. 'This is nuts' he thinks, heading back along the path.

"MAUREEN!" he calls out. He stops still to listen. Nothing. His heart thumps as with all the other times. He is about halfway along the path when he turns to run back to the hotel, before tripping over and landing flat on his face. A sound from behind, he looks over, nothing, only children's laughter filling the air. The laughter getting louder and closer as he clambers up and sprints up the steps and heads to the entrance. He slams the double doors open and closes them behind him, staring back through the glass. He is panting like a dog, concentrating on the outside. 'I'm going crazy, I'm seeing things' he thinks. Then, a pat on the back out of nowhere.

"FOR FUCKS SAKE!" he cries out, before turning to see a very startled Clare.

"What has happened to you?" she asks him, started to see her new boss soaked to the bone, blood pouring out of his nose, covered in soggy leaf litter and pond muck, a mix of rotting feathers, and putrefied leaf litter.

"And that awful smell?" she said. He looks back around, staring out through the window. He is fully expecting to see a woman and some children walk through the rose covered archway. But nobody comes.

"Come on, get inside, you need a ruddy shower," she tells him, in her usual assertive manner.

"I need a bloody drink, get me a double, please!" he orders. Clare looks shocked as Archie hurries over from his wire repairs at reception.

"What's gone on laddie?" he asks.

"Don't ask, honestly, I'm losing my shit here!" he said.

"Why, was it the kids you're hearing?" he asks. Clare comes back with a long bath towel and wraps it around him. He is shivering profusely, a combination of the cold and shock.

"Tell us, why are you drenched?" asks Archie.

"The pond, I fell in the bloody thing; nearly drowned. Then an old woman helped me out." Archie and Clare look at each other, as Bruce still peers over to the entrance doors.

"A woman by the pond you say?" asks Clare.

"That's what I said, good job she was around; I owe my life to her!"

Clare walked over to Culloden room, briefly disappearing, before reappearing with a bottle of lager.

"Here, it's all there is in the bar at the moment." she says and hands him the bottle. He swigs it at first and then almost downs the whole thing, dribbles running down his muddies cheeks.

"Did you get a name?" asks Archie.

"I did, Aline I think," he said.

"Aline?" he asks

"Do you mean Maureen?"

"That's it, yes, it was Maureen, sure as a fart farts!" he jokes. Archie was about to tell him a little more about a 'Maureen,' but Clare tapped him on the shoulder, shaking her head. Bruce dries himself off as best he could. The hot water in the hotel was a bit hit and miss still, so headed back to his private quarters, where there's a decent electric power shower. Meanwhile, Clare and Archie head into the back office where they start to discuss what he had seen and heard.

"Maureen?" asks Clare

"Aye, I heard him, she must be back?"

"But why, she drowned in the pond years ago, why now?" asks Clare. She knew of the story and a lot more on top.

"It must be the bloodline, everything is getting stirred up," said Archie.

"What, the family bloodline?" she asks. Archie walks over to the window and stares out across the front driveway.

"I have never seen this before. His arrival here, from day one has awoken something. Something that Alice and his mother had dabbled with here!"

"So, they sense it's in his bloodline, I get it now," said Clare.

"What can we do about it?" asks Archie.

"That's easy, you have to leave the reinstatement of room 19 off for a while longer. Magda will have to do her thing, or we are all doomed here." It so happens that Magda the housekeeper is a member of the spiritualist church that Alice attended. On more than one occasion she had joined Alice in room 19, as Alice desperately tried to contact Stanley. She knew how to conduct the perfect séance. Bruce hurries down the grand staircase and leans on the reception counter, feeling revived and much better. For now, at least, his nose had stopped bleeding. Fortunately, he had brought the boxes containing his clothes, and he had thrown on a dry set of clothes. They come out to see him.

"There, that's better, all tidy and dry," said Clare.

"Yep, I feel better now, just can't explain the day's events," he said.

She placed a hand on his shoulder and said:

"Sometimes things are unexplainable."

"He smiled at her and agreed, before heading off with haste to the corridor leading to the kitchen. Archie appears from the Culloden room.

"You ok now Pal?" he asks.

"Fine, at the moment, this place is something else, right?"

"She's a wonder for sure, and she senses that we are bringing her back to life." They chat a little longer and Archie asks him to go into the cellar to check a fuse board and a couple of boilers. Bruce refuses and explains that he'd had enough for one day. The bottle of lager was already giving him a headache, causing him to feel tired. He arranged to come back on Monday to help with cutting the grass while the new team got on with taking calls, hopefully leading to bookings. Archie said he would pop in on Sunday to finish off the telephone lines. He arranged to be back for 9am Monday.

On route home, he stopped into a carwash to get rid of the so-called graffiti on his car. As usual after a visit to the hotel, the events he witnessed filled his head with all the usual thoughts. Although most of them were creepy and unexplainable, he had a fond feeling for the place. It was starting to feel like home and his house was starting to feel less so. That feeling was intensifying each day, especially with the passing of his nosey neighbour. That evening at home, he finished off sorting a few more things out. The more he got done, the better, although most of the bulky boxes were now at Dunella. The man and van was due mid-week, to take the rest of everything there. Namely his bicycle, his shed equipment and the rest of his belongings.

The day was coming to a close. He was so exhausted that he hadn't given it a thought to take a shower after his somewhat smelly experience in the pond. As he got into bed, the thoughts came flooding back. Kids voices, weird graffiti, disappearing Maureen. He stares at the ceiling again, processing it all. He checks the time, almost midnight, dozing in and out of sleep until: THUD! THUD! THUD! "Holy shit!" he says out loud, sitting up and staring at the opposite wall, neighbours' side. This time is a bit different. In anticipation for the banging to happen again, he slips back down under the covers, staring at the offending wall. 'THUD! THUD! THUD!'

"PISS OFF JIMMEY!" he cries out.

The next morning, he awoke later than usual. Apart from the now strange pattern of knocking coming from his deceased neighbour's house, it was just another typical Sunday morning. One thing was for sure; he wouldn't be taking a trip to creepy Claypotts like he did last Sunday. Today was all about finishing off the packing.

# Chapter ten

He was feeling upbeat about sorting his things out. He felt it was a good idea to have a shower, considering he hadn't bothered last night. He knew it was going to be one of the last ones in the house. The shower was just what the doctor ordered. After feeling refreshed and heaping plenty of shaving foam on, he noticed something else. It was a reminder that things were not always explainable. The gash on his head that occurred after the fall jogging. It was healed in a miraculous manner at Claypotts. Not long after it reappeared again. This morning, it was completely gone.

He made sure the usual breakfast was made, porridge with plenty honey on the top. The key addition as usual a cup of coffee, with three heaped teaspoons of coffee and four teaspoons of sugar. It was time to revert to an old habit. The weather was bright and had not rained. So, it was time for a jog. The same practice as ever, carefully leaving his front door, peering around the corner to make sure the close was clear. 'Silly sod,' he thought, remembering that the coast would always be clear, now that Jimmey was gone.

Off he went, striding at a steady pace across the road and into the mouth of the pathway There was nobody around and he can recall only ever stopping to see Jimmey if he was out walking Loki. He felt sad, as he carried on deeper along the pathway. His slip and fall, very much in mind along with the strange vision while he was unconscious. What was 'Nuts' trying to tell him. A warning from beyond the grave? And the cyclist who helped him home, Pat, who or what was he? He was starting to question his mental wellbeing. When certain strange things present themselves to you in life, we often question them. It is true that if someone sees a ghost, the other sees just a shadow or trick of the light. One thing was for sure; he couldn't rubbish the terrifying sighting of the green lady, witnessed by not just himself, but Archie too.

He was almost home, reaching the road opposite his house. He stared over at the dull, quiet appearance that was Jimmey's house. He stopped at the roads edge and took a few breaths, trying to get his breath.

'THUD! THUD! THUD!' He could clearly hear, the sound eerily resonating around the place. He looked up at the front bedroom window, aware that this was the source of the same noise at night. It happened once more. 'THUD! THUD! THUD!' he looked up. There stood in the window, was a shadow, a form of a person. The body was see-through, like a restful fog, dark grey. No features, but just like the one he saw when he first went to Dunella, it was undeniable. He froze, looking up at the window, chills running up and down his spine.

"What are you?" he says quietly, observing, trying to understand, not rejecting the image or branding the form as 'imaginary.' He walks slowly over to the other side of the road and concentrates on the figure. It is still, silent, no thuds, just staring him out. There wasn't a single sound apart from his thump! Thump! of the heart pounding faster in his chest. And then:

"Morning Mr!" He almost jumped out of skin, as he moved aside to allow a young canvasser access to Jimmey's gate. He was briefly interrupted. He looked back up and the image was gone.

"You ok Mr?" asked the canvasser.

"Why wouldn't I be?" he replied.

"Oh, nothing, you look like you've seen a ghost that's all buddy," he said, handing him a 'Vote Lyndsay Sayer' Labour leaflet. He said nothing else and went inside. He felt better for the morning jog, but that image was eating away at him. He put on fresh clothes and started to finish off his packing. He had a foreboding feeling that although strange things were going on at Dunella, his sanctuary at home was also presenting him with creepy visions and sounds. By early afternoon, he was finished. Everything was ready to go with the man and van due Wednesday. He had decided that this coming night would be the last one. Tomorrow he would stay at Dunella.

Monday arrived. Thankfully, the wall Thud noises abated, as if the vision was his neighbour's soul saying a final goodbye. That thought creeped the shit out of him. He was between a rock and a hard place. He knew that eventually he had to stay for good at the hotel. Tonight was no time like the right time. If he was going to be involved cutting grass and overseeing the efforts with promotions, he wanted to be there. The military house would remain his for a few more weeks anyway. He left a key to the front door in a secret place, texting the details to the 'man and van.'

He set off with a few items on-board, leaving the bulk of boxes and tools and bicycle for the final delivery mid-week. He already had the essentials up in the PS along with all his personal artefacts. He arrived at the driveway, heading around slowly to his usual parking spot, just opposite reception. This time, the place was alive. There were three vans in the carpark to the left, just before the rose covered archway. Gas services, electrical services and an internet company. There were a couple of bicycles in the stand and a few other cars here and there. 'This is more like it,' he thought. He headed inside.

The reception lobby was crawling with people, scurrying from left to right, noise from a drill or two and the clang of cutlery. Dunella had come to life. He could see Clare at reception, going over something with Katey. There was an BT engineer there too, fiddling around, liaising with Archie. He said nothing to them, just waved, letting him know he was there, and headed off through to the lift corridor for the trolley. He noticed toolboxes scattered around, the odd reel of wire and the kitchen door at the far end was propped open. He found the trolley; it had been put outside the double fire escape doors. He heads out to put a few bits onto it. Noting that it was so far so good, no children from wherever goading and heckling him. Archie pops out.

"Morning Pal," he says.

"Hi, lots going on then."

"Yup, boilers getting serviced, a few gas hob niggles in the kitchen and I had to call BT in. They are sorting the lines and internet out as we speak," he said. Bruce placed a box on the trolley, just as a large van pulled in. "Oh, the whole town is coming today," he said.

"Ha seems like it, that's the linen company, Magda arranged delivery for today. And then two more vehicles pulled into the drive. One large van bringing a valuable food delivery, followed closely by a lorry from the local brewery.

"I don't know what I would have done without you all Archie, I mean that. Archie thanked him briefly and headed off to see the van driver. He called over "GRASS CUTTING IN A WEE WHILE OK!" That was it, orders given. In the madness that was going on,

Bruce and Archie would add to the chaos outside. The time had come. Bruce finally got the rest of his things upstairs. He felt much better that he would be there to stay. He managed to have a quick chat with the ladies and Archie updated him with the trades onsite and their progress. It had got to about mid-day and it was time to be introduced to the lawn mower. In the grounds was a small shed, about 8 feet x ten feet in size. It looked like it had been repaired several times, with mismatching bits of wood here and there. Inside revealed a plethora of gardening tools. Slap bang in the centre was a bright red lawn mower.

"Right, this is Madge, the mad mower," said Archie.

"Madge, right, how come it's got a name?"

"Och, it's a trend that stuck aroond here, a certain gardener named everything and all her equipment, said Archie.

"You mean Maureen?" said Bruce. Archie looked at him and nodded, saying nothing, instead changing the subject.

"I filled her up, fresh petrol, all good, stand back. He switched on the ignition, illuminating a panel in the gloom. Then, he yanked on a pull chord. Madge fired up, filling the shed with blue and grey smoke.

"Ignore that, it will clear, she needs to warm up a wee bit," said Archie. He backed out the shed, proudly mounted atop Madge. After a ten-minute induction, Bruce sat on her and gave it a go. With further orders from Archie, he carefully set off and soon he was up and down the main lawn, chopping away at the overly long grass. He enjoyed it a lot. It gave him time to think about all sorts and in a strange way it was very relaxing. Archie had headed back inside to oversee the works going on.

After a couple more hours and at least one refill of petrol, Bruce had mown the whole rear lawn. He stood proudly just by the rear ponds, admiring his efforts. The fine day enthused with the smell of freshly cut grass really refreshed his senses. At that point, he hadn't even given a thought to the incident that almost caused his drowning. It was time to go inside, in search of coffee and fast, he was gasping for his usual caffeine dose. He noticed one of two brewery guys that had been loading all sorts of lager bottles and beer kegs into the cellar. One of which had sorted all the beer lines behind the bar, giving the pumps a quick once over. The fat one that had been down in the cellar was leaning on his knees, as if gasping for a breath. He went over to see what was up.

"You ok big man?" he asked. He shook his head.

"I won't be going down there again Mr; this place is full of spirits!"

"The drinking type you mean?" said Bruce in jest. The big brewery man stood up and looked directly at him.

"Mate, I used to come here, years back and I promised myself never to return. That bloody cellar is hell on earth!" he said, it never gets any better," he said, as he stepped up into the lorry cab.

"What happened, what did you see?" asked Bruce. The man started the engine, shaking his head and said:

"You don't want to see it, put it that way, this hotel, its cursed!" he said and started to drive away. Bruce thought the day had gone really well and was determined not to let that snippet of creepy information upset his day. He was almost inside the reception lobby, when a grimy engineer scurried past him, toolbox in hand. It was the BT engineer. And, on a positive note, just a second or two later, the sound of a telephone rang out.

"YAY!" he could here Clare shout out. And then another followed by: Good afternoon, Dunella hotel, how may I help You." The rest of the day passed by without incident. Most of the work was sorted apart from a few electrical jobs in bedrooms. The electrician would be there all week, working from room to room, creating an electrical report, fixing minor issues as he went. Thankfully, Archie had kept on top of the plumbing around the hotel. The gas service was completed and signed off. The telephones kept on ringing. The atmosphere had changed entirely. Magda was darting all over the place like a rash with two young housekeepers sorting out all the bedding, room by room.

They had cleaned and vacuumed the main reception earlier, making the musty smell completely disappear. Eventually, the flurry of activity calmed down. Clare and Archie left together, and the rest of the staff, including Magda left for home. It was about 5.30pm and for the first time, he was alone. Back inside the hotel, he wandered around reception, admiring the spotless check-in counter. It was so clean, he could see his face, warts and all, in the shiny reflection. There was a fresh smell all around, a combination of polish and lemons. He noticed a checklist on the counter that Clare had left behind. It was a long list; each one had a big tick at the end. From gas service to Beer lines, all the important things you would expect to get a hotel back up and running. He thought to have a nosey inside the back office.

Inside, he could see another few changes. The desk was moved around to face the window, enabling the seated party to look out at the drive. There were two white boards up. Archie had been very busy. On one of the two boards, he could see something very positive. The number 15 followed by 'Booking confirmations' He felt a sense of excitement when he read that. After all, the business had to do well to support all the wages, deliveries etc. All of which he was still in the dark about. He hadn't even been asked at that point about supporting such things with his money.

There was also something else on the desk. He had a nosey at that too. It was a form for the staff to sign in and sign out for that day. Obviously, they were being paid for their time. He noted that they had all signed in, Archie at the top, Clare, Magda, Katey and the housekeepers. The only names not signed out were Clare, Magda and Archie, the others had done so. He thought nothing of it and put it down, making sure it was where it had been. He left the office.

    He started to feel relaxed about the place, wandering around, noting all the changes made. It such a short period of time, all was getting done so well. There was a strong smell of paint all around, just from Archie touching up the place. He started to wonder if Archie had had time to sort out room 19, so that was next on the list to check out. He climbed up the grand staircase and to the corridor with room 19. There wasn't much to see. The hasp and staple were still in position, but the padlock was missing. The door was locked, and he didn't have a clue where that key was. He looked up and down, pushing the door. He placed an ear to it. He thought he could hear something, a voice or two. He leaned in closer, listening in. Something sounded like a footstep and then, there was silence. He waited for a minute or two, but nothing else happened.

    The day had been extremely busy, so it was a relief when he headed off up the rear stairs to his own corridor. He shortly arrived at his new home to be, the private suite. It was getting later in the evening now. Housekeeping didn't have time to get up there, but it was already clean and tidy. He definitely wanted to try out the fancy bath. And in no time at all, thanks to the gas engineers, the bath was filled with hot soapy water. He plunged himself into it, reeling back for a moment as the hot water stung his toes.

It seemed like ages in that bath. He had no reason to rush it. It was the most relaxing thing he had done for months. He really was feeling grateful, up on top of a Georgian hotel that he owned. Plenty money in the bank and a business too. The future was looking great. Granted, he knew all was a bit 'unusual' to say the least about the place. However, with his strength of mind, with his experiences in the army over some 30 years, it wasn't impacting him like it would do the normal man in the street. At least not yet...

He jumped out of the bath, noticing it was starting to get gloomy outside. He switched on the TV on top of a fancy stand and sat down in his dressing gown. He flicked through the channels, arriving at BBC 1, just in time for the 9 o'clock news. The report was about another British fatality in Afghanistan. One of the provinces he had been to and fought in himself. The very place he left his best friend 'nuts' behind. He suddenly felt shame creep over him. There he was Lording it up, in a fancy pad atop his hotel after a steaming hot bath. And somewhere over there in one of the worlds worse shit holes, a young soldier was being zipped up ready for a grim journey home. He hung his head in his hands and started to weep. He couldn't stop, an emotion crept over him, the type only a soldier can understand.

And then suddenly, a noise. He looks up. He listens, still as a Lizard. "You slut!" said a man's voice. He noticed that there was an American tone to it. Immediately followed by a scream. The sounds were muffled as if coming from below or up through an open window. He freezes, wondering where to look.

"No, please, I can explain!" said a woman's voice, this time with a Scottish accent. He hears a scuffle, a bang and another noise. A scream, a man's voice and then silence.

"I told you bitch, you are mine, all mine, no one else touches you," said the American voice. The scuffle continues, from the floor below. At least it seemed to be from there.

"NO! NO! Don't do it, I love you!" said the woman. Bruce is walking back and forth, wondering if someone has left a play on or a TV. One thing is for sure; he is startled.

"You are mine for all eternity you bitch,"he hears again, followed by a dull muffled thud sound, then another, and another. As this is going on the womans screams die down eventually stopping. Bruce throws on his jeans and trainers and pulls on a Tee Shirt. He goes over to the window, listening and looking. No sound. No one. He has to have a look downstairs. He knows that beneath him is the corridor with room 19. He didn't want to believe it. He opened the door and made his way to the back stairs, trying to ignore the whistling sound. That seemed like nothing compared to what he had just heard. He didn't know it, but that was the replay of Tobias murdering Shirley. But how and why?

He walked along the corridor and could see a light flickering under the door. He stopped and looked down. He could hear talking, louder than before. He touched the brass door handle, like a child who creeps into a sibling's room at night. It seemed like ages. The talking and chatter getting louder. He looked along the corridor left and right, in disbelief that only a few minutes ago, he was sat recovering from a hot bath, and now he was stood outside dreaded room 19, bathed in total terror.

Then, the door bursts open, and he is pulled inside by a force unseen. He tries to stop himself being pulled in further, clutching onto the doorframe. But it's no good, he's pulled inside, he looks down, to see his feet are above the floor, floating. He screams out in terror, looking around in blind panic as he floats across the lobby to the door leading into the room with the round table.

He tries to scream again but this time, his voice is muted. He sees people sat at the table. He can't believe his eyes. Through the gaps between people, he can see tall candle's flickering and a mist swirling around the room. The temperature has dropped to a cool few degrees above freezing. He stops, still floating, observing, shivering and terrorised. He stares across at the table, seeing them all holding hands, dressed in black robes, chanting. A chant he didn't understand or want to. One woman, he recognised, and another. The unmistakable Archie looks around at him too. His eyes wide, whites only and fluttering!

"CLARE WHAT THE FUCK!" he screams. She turns to look at him, her eyes fluttering around, pure white, and they stare at him. Then she says: "Hi darling, long time no see, lovely to see you again, "she said, only to his utter shock horror, that voice was that of his late departed mother. The other lady joined in staring at him, eyes wide, white and fluttering saying: "Hi laddie, you are so missed, I'm so sorry about how I left you." she said in the unmistakable voice of his father, Alec. Bruce can't believe his eyes, he wonders if he's dreaming as his voice returns allowing him to scream.

"WHAT THE...OH MY FUCK...ARCHIE!... LET ME THE HELL OUT!"

He can't move, the misty fog around the room gathers onto the middle of the table. As it does so, it seems to take on form. A couple struggling. He stares at this sight watching as the mist became a recognisable form. It is woman with dark hair holding onto an elderly man, as she tries to fight him off. Then he sees a weapon, the axe swinging up and down, several times. His heart is pounding. Suddenly the apparition screams and then falls silent. The remaining one of the two, the man, is peering down at her. This whole scene was seared into his mind. He prays to be released and suddenly, his feet touch the floor.

"FUCK THIS!" he shouts as he turns to run out to the corridor. The door is closed, he fights the handle, pulling it with all his might, looking over his shoulder. The chants continue and the misty form leaves the table. Its heading his way. By now, Bruce is wondering why he hasn't passed out. The door opens, he turns to run along the corridor, but there are two apparitions stood at the end. He turns and runs the other way, back to the rear whistling stairwell.

'Thank fuck he thinks' assuming the stairwell is clear. He starts to head down, but is met with another pair of eerie souls, approaching up the stairs. He starts to head down, but he's met with another pair of eerie souls, silently floating up the stairs. He turns around, leaping up three steps at a time, the only way is to the PS.

He bursts through the door and slams it behind him, desperately trying to grab a breath. In panic he goes into the kitchen and pulls out a bread knife. "What the fuck now?" he said to himself. Without warning, the front door rattles. It doesn't stop, it increases, vibrating, louder and then it bursts open. He runs through into the lounge, feeling slight relief to see his window open, from when he was looking around for the noise source.

And then, with no warning he sees the stuff of nightmares. The terrifying form that left the table was stood at the doorway and dropped something on the floor. It just stood there, motionless. It started to take form, all the mist and fog replaced with pigment and colour. The item on the floor was a bloodied axe. Bruce is frozen stiff, heart pounding, the room temperature freezing. He is beside himself with utter terror. The only way out now is the window. He pulls it up further and starts to climb out. He has one leg over the window ledge, hoping to step out onto a ledge he can see in the moonlight. He is stuck; he looks aback into the room. As he does so the man rushes to the window and stops, seeming to peer down, not noticing him at all. Bruce freezes, looking right at him, not daring to move, one leg outside.

"Bitch, she knew what I was like. There's no alternative." he spoke in an American accent. From behind him, inside the room came a terrifying voice, snarly and raspy saying:

"Jump you loser, do it! do it! go on, jump and I'll meet you in hell!"

The window raised further and caused Bruce to lose his grip. He had nothing to hold on to. The man climbed out and leapt from the window ledge, silently plunging into the moonlit night. Bruce tried to cling on, but his fingers slipped on the cool night's condensation on the paintwork. He slips and falls backwards. As he hurtles to the ground, he sees the hotel ebbing and flowing as he swirled through the air. And then: blackness. He had fallen to the ground, following the cursed path that Tobias had taken.

"Bruce, can you hear me?" a calming voice said. It was a doctor, checking his vital signs. He opens one eye and focuses in on the ceiling. As if by a miracle, he had landed on a delivery of plants and bags of mulch that Archie had ordered. He had still broken four ribs, an arm and his left leg. His internal bleeding was a worry, but after three days in an induced coma, his vital signs were improving. It is unknown who called 999 but it came from the hotel. He was in a bad way and lucky to be alive. He had tubes coming out of every orifice, but he was sedated, stable and had survived. The doctor asks again.

"How are you feeling, squeeze my hand if you can," she asks. He grabs her hand and squeezes, managing to spew out a few words.

"How am I feeling?...swinging off the chandelier me," he replies and falls back to sleep.

"Bruce, can you hear me?" a calming voice said. It was a doctor, checking his vital signs. As if by a miracle, he had landed on a delivery of plants and bags of mulch that Archie had ordered. He had still broken four ribs, an arm and both legs. His internal bleeding was a worry, but after three days in an induced coma, his vital signs were improving. It is unknown who called 999 but it came from the hotel. He was in a bad way and lucky to be alive. He had tubes coming out of every orifice, but he was sedated, stable and had survived.

The following Monday morning at reception, a young family arrived for a short break, heading inside to check in. As if nothing at all had happened, Clare came out of the office to greet her first guests.

"Hello, welcome to Dunella!"

## *The end???*

Printed in Great Britain
by Amazon